'You've been thinking about me, too.' He caught her hand, held it in a relaxed grip.

'No.'

His thumb whisked over her knuckles. 'Admit it, Emma.'

She made one final, albeit half-hearted attempt to pull away, but his gaze held hers and he lifted her hand to his chest. His heart thumped strong and deep.

'You've been wondering about our first kiss all day,' he continued in that low, seductive tone. 'Like when...'

Still massaging the base of her scalp, he leaned in, touched warm, firm lips to hers. *Oh, my.*

'And where...'

Heat flowed like honey as he slid the tip of his tongue over her bottom lip.

'And how...'

When not teaching or writing, **Anne Oliver** loves nothing more than escaping into a book. She keeps a box of tissues handy—her favourite stories are intense, passionate, against-all-odds romances. Eight years ago she began creating her own characters in paranormal and time travel adventures, before turning to contemporary romance. Other interests include quilting, astronomy, all things Scottish, and eating anything she doesn't have to cook. Sharing her characters' journeys with readers all over the world is a privilege…and a dream come true. Anne lives in Adelaide, South Australia, and has two adult children. Visit her website at www.anne-oliver.com She loves to hear from readers. E-mail her at anne@anne-oliver.com

Recent titles by the same author:

**Did you know these are also available as eBooks?
Visit www.millsandboon.co.uk**

THE MORNING AFTER THE WEDDING BEFORE

BY
ANNE OLIVER

MILLS
BOON

First published in Great Britain 2012
by Mills & Boon, an imprint of Harlequin (UK) Limited.
Harlequin (UK) Limited, Eton House, 18-24 Paradise Road,
Richmond, Surrey TW9 1SR

© Anne Oliver 2012

ISBN: 978 0 263 22719 2

Harlequin (UK) policy is to use papers that are natural, renewable
and recyclable products and made from wood grown in sustainable
forests. The logging and manufacturing process conform to the
legal environmental regulations of the country of origin.

Printed and bound in Great Britain
by CPI Antony Rowe, Chippenham, Wiltshire

THE MORNING AFTER THE WEDDING BEFORE

To Sue.
You're loyal, generous, compassionate and caring,
touching people's lives in the best way, and a
true friend on life's amazing and unpredictable journey.

Thank you for always being there! Anne

CHAPTER ONE

Emma Byrne refused to give in to the nerves zapping beneath her ribcage like hysterical wasps. She was a sophisticated city girl, she wasn't afraid of walking into a third-rate strip club. Alone.

But she paused on the footpath in King's Cross, Sydney's famous nightclub district, and racked her brain for an alternative solution as she eyed the bruiser of a bouncer propped against the tacky-looking entrance.

Six p.m. on a balmy autumn Monday evening and the Pink Mango was already open for business. Sleazy business. She gulped down the insane urge to laugh—she'd been naïve enough to think the Pink Mango was an all-night deli.

But she'd promised her sister she'd deliver the best man's suit to Jake Carmody, and she would. She could.

Pushing the big sunglasses she'd found in her glove box farther up her nose, she slung her handbag and the plastic suit bag over one stiff shoulder and marched inside. The sound system's get-your-gear-off bump and grind pounded through hidden speakers. The place smelled like beer and cheap cologne and smut. Her nostrils flared in distaste as she drew in a reluctant breath.

Her steps faltered as a zillion eyes seemed to look her way. *You're imagining it,* she told herself. *Who'd give you a second glance in a dive like this?* Especially given her knee-length buttoned-up red trench coat, knee-high boots and leather gloves, all of which she'd left on the back seat of her car since last winter. Which, when she thought about it, could very well be the reason she was garnering more than a few stares…

Better safe than sorry. Thank heavens for untidy cars and a convenient parking spot.

Ignoring the curious eyes, she turned her attention to the décor instead. The interior was even tackier than the outside. Cheap lolly pink and gold and black. The chairs and couches were covered in a dirty-looking fuchsia animal print. A revolving disco ball spewed gaudy colours over the circulating topless waitresses with smiles as fake as their boobs.

At least they *had* boobs.

Most of the early-evening punters were lounging around a raised oval stage leering over their drinks at a lone female dancer wearing nothing but a fuzzy gold string and making love to a brass pole. A hooded cobra was tattooed on one firm butt cheek.

Far out. Despite herself, Emma couldn't seem to tear her fascinated gaze away. *What men like…* She'd never have that voluptuousness, nor the chutzpah to carry it off.

Maybe that was the reason Wayne had called it quits.

Shaking off the self-doubt, she blew out a deep, slow breath and turned away from the entertainment. Just what she *didn't* need right now. A reminder of her physical inadequacies.

I don't care if you and Ryan are getting married next weekend, little sister, you owe me big-time for doing this.

'I've got an appointment to get my nails done,' Stella had told her with more than a touch of pre-wedding desperation in her voice. 'Ryan's in Melbourne for a conference till tomorrow and you don't have anything special on tonight, do you?'

Stella knew Emma had no social life whatsoever since the break-up with Wayne. Of course she'd be free. Wouldn't have mattered if she wasn't. As the maid of honour, how could she refuse the bride's request? But a strip joint had *not* been part of the deal.

A man in an open shirt with a thick gold chain over an obscene mat of greying chest hair watched her from behind a desk nearby. His flat, penetrating gaze—as if he was imagining her naked and finding her not up to par—made her stomach heave. A bead of sweat trickled down her back—it was stifling inside this coat.

But he seemed to be the obvious person to speak to, so she moved quickly. She straightened her spine and forced herself to look him in the eyes. Not easy when those eyes were staring at her chest.

But before she got a word out he twirled one fat finger and said, 'If you've come about the job, take off that coat and show us what you've got.'

The hairs on the back of her neck prickled and, appalled, she tightened her belt. 'I *beg* your pardon? I'm n—'

'You won't need a costume here, darlin',' he drawled, eyeing the garment bag over her shoulder. 'We're one down tonight so you can start on the tables. Cherry'll show you. Oi, Cherry!' His smoke-scratched voice blasted through the thick air.

Emma cringed as people looked their way, glad of her dark glasses. She summoned her frostiest tone. 'I'm here to speak to Jake Carmody.'

He shook his head. 'Won't make a scrap of difference, y'know. Seen plenty just like you pass through the door hiding behind a disguise, expecting to make a quick buck on the side.'

'*Excuse me?* Just tell me where I can find Mr Carmody so I can finish my business with him and be *out of here*.'

Those pale flat eyes checked her out some more as a woman approached toting a tray of drinks. She was wearing eighties gold hot pants and a transparent black blouse. Beneath her make-up Emma saw that she looked drawn and tired and felt a stirring of sympathy. She knew all about working jobs out of sheer necessity, and was grateful she'd never been quite so desperate.

'Lady here wants to see the boss. Know where he is?'

The boss? 'There must be some mistake…' Emma trailed off. His PA had told her she'd find him at this address, but…he was the *boss* of this dive?

The woman called Cherry gave a weary half shrug. 'In the office, last I saw.'

He jerked a thumb at a narrow staircase on the far side of the room. 'Up the stairs, first door on the right.'

'Thank you.' Lips pressed together, and aware of a few gazes following her, she made her way through the club, keeping as far away from the action as possible.

The *boss?*

Despite the heat, she shivered inside her coat. His lifestyle was none of her business, but she'd never in a million years have expected the guy she remembered to be involved in a lower-than-low strip joint. He already had a career, didn't he? A degree in business law, for goodness' sake. *Please don't let him have chucked in years of study and a respectable livelihood for this…*

Sleaze Central's business obviously paid better. Money over morals.

She knew Jake from high school. He was one of Ryan's mates, and the two guys had often turned up at home to catch up with her more sociable sister and listen to music. Emma had been either working one of her after-school jobs or experimenting with her soap-making, but there'd been a few times when Stella had persuaded her to chill out with them.

Jake the Rake, Emma had privately thought him. A chick magnet. Totally cool, ever so slightly dangerous, and way too experienced for a girl like her. Maybe that was why she'd always tried to avoid him whenever possible.

Hadn't stopped her from being a little in love with him, though. She shook it away. Obviously her young eyes had been clouded by naïveté and love was definitely not in her life plan. Not ever again.

She heard him before she reached the door. That familiar deep, somewhat lazy voice that seemed to roll over the senses like thick caramel sauce. She *was* well and truly over her youthful crush on him, wasn't she? He was on the phone, and as she paused to listen his tone changed from laid-back to harassed.

The door was open a crack and she knocked. She heard a clatter as he slammed the phone down, a short, succinct rude word and then an impatient, 'Come in.'

He didn't look up straight away, which gave her a moment to slide her sunglasses on top of her head and look him over.

Sitting at a shabby desk littered with papers, he was writing something, head bent over a file. He wore a sky-blue shirt, open at the neck, sleeves rolled up over sinewy bronzed forearms. Unlike the rest of this dive, his clothing was top of the line. Her gaze lifted to his face and her heart pattered that tiny bit faster. God's gift with a sinner's lips...

An unnerving little shiver ran through her and she jerked her eyes higher. His rich, dark hair was sticking up in short tufts here and there, as if he'd been ploughing his hands through it. Her fingers itched to smooth it down—

Good grief, she was lusting after a man who owned a seedy striptease venue—a man who not only used women but exploited them. Wanting to touch him made her as low as him and as bad as those pervs downstairs. But, despite her best efforts to ignore them, little quivers continued to reverberate up and down the length of her spine.

'Hello, Jake.' She impressed herself with her aloof greeting and only wished she felt as cool.

He glanced up. His frown was replaced by stunned surprise. As if he'd been caught in a shop window with his made-to-measure pants down. She blinked the disconcerting image away.

'Emma.' Putting his pen down slowly, he closed the file he'd been working on, took his sweet time to stand—all six-foot-plus of gorgeous male—and said, 'Long time no see.'

'Yes,' she agreed, ignoring the tantalising glimpse of masculine hair visible at the neck of his shirt, the way his broad shoulders shifted against the fabric. 'Well…we've all got busy lives.'

'Yeah, it's all go these days isn't it? Unlike high school.' He came round to the side of the desk with a smile that was like a lingering caress and did amazing tingly things to her body.

She took a step back. She needed to get out. Fast. 'I can see you're busy,' she hurried on, keeping her gaze focused on his black coffee eyes. 'I j—'

'Are you here for a job?'

What? She felt her jaw drop, and for a moment she simply stared while her brain played catch-up and heat crawled up her neck. The sod. The dirty rotten *sod.* 'I phoned your office—your *other* office—and your PA told me you were here.'

Her lip curled on the last word and she tossed the garment bag onto the desk, sending papers flying every which way. 'Your suit for the wedding. If it needs altering the tailor says he needs at least three days' notice, which is why I'm dropping it off tonight. Ryan's interstate, and Stella had an appointment, so I—'

'Emma. I was joking.'

Oh. She glimpsed the twinkle in his eye and took another step back. Twinkles were dangerous. And why wouldn't he joke? Because no way did she measure up to those voluptuous creatures downstairs. 'I don't have time to joke today. Or anything else. So…um…you've got the suit. I'll be off, then.'

He watched her a moment longer, as if saying *What's your hurry?* Beneath the harsh single fluorescent light she saw the bruised smudges and feathery lines of stress around his eyes, as if he hadn't slept in weeks.

Well, good, she thought. He deserved to be stressed for making her feel like an inadequate fool. As if her self-esteem wasn't suffering enough after Wayne ending their relationship, and in this place…

'So, it's *Gone with the Wind* for us two, eh? Hope I can do Rhett Butler justice.' He glanced at the bag, then aimed that sexy grin at her. 'And you're to be my Scarlett for the day.'

She stiffened at the darkly delicious—no, *bad* thought. But her blood pulsed a bit more heavily through her body. 'I'm not your anyone. Why they had to choose a famous couples-themed wedding's beyond me.'

He shrugged. 'They wanted something sparkling and original and wildly romantic—and why not? Might as well have some fun on the big day. Everything's downhill from there.' His long, sensuous fingers curled around the edge of the desk and he aimed that killer smile again. 'Thanks for dropping it off. Can I get you a drink before you leave?'

Good heavens. 'No. Thank you.'

Crossing his arms, Jake leaned a hip against the desk, inhaling the fresh, unfamiliar fragrance that had swirled in with her. She was an energising sight for tired eyes. What he could see of her.

Tall and slim as a blue-eyed poppy. Even angry she looked amazing, with that ice-cold sapphire gaze and that way she had of pouting her lips. All glossy and plump and…

He fought a sudden mad impulse to walk over and taste them. Probably shouldn't have made that wisecrack about a job here. But he'd not been able to resist getting a rise out of her. On the few occasions she'd been persuaded to join them she'd always been so damn serious. Obviously that hadn't changed.

The muffled thump from downstairs vibrated through the floor. He rasped his hands over his stubbled jaw. 'If I'd known you were coming I'd've arranged for you to drop the suit at my office. My *other* office.'

She drilled him some more with that icy stare. And he felt oddly bruised, as if she'd punched him in the gut with her…gloved hand.

'I have to go,' she said stiffly.

He pushed off the desk. 'I'll walk you down.'

'No. I'd really rather you didn't.'

The tone. He knew well enough not to mess with it and crossed his arms. 'Okay. Thanks again for dropping the suit by. Appreciate it.'

'Glad to hear that, because it's a one-off.'

'I'll see you tomorrow night at the wedding dinner.'

'Seven-thirty.' She hitched her bag higher. 'Don't be late.'

'Emma...' She glanced back and he thought once again of poppies. About lying in a field of them on a summer's day. With Emma. 'It's good to see you again.'

She didn't reply, but she did hesitate, staring at him with those fabulous eyes and allowing him to indulge in the cheerful poppy fantasy a few seconds longer. And he could have sworn he felt a...*zap.* Then she nodded once and her head snapped back to the doorway.

He watched her leave, admiring the way she moved, all straight and sexy and *classy.* He wondered for a moment why he'd never pursued anything with her back in the day. He'd seen her look his way more than once when she'd thought he wasn't watching.

His lingering smile dropped away. He knew why. Emma Byrne didn't know the meaning of fun, and she certainly didn't know how to chill out. She wore *serious* the way other women wore designer jeans.

Jake, on the other hand, didn't do serious. He didn't do commitment. He enjoyed women—on his terms. Women who knew the score. And when it was over it was over, no misunderstandings. No looking back. But, *hoo-yeah...* He couldn't deny this lovely, more mature, more womanly Emma turned him on. Big time.

The door closed and he listened to her footsteps fade, stretching his arms over his head, imagining her walking downstairs. In that neck-to-ankle armour—which only added to the sexual intrigue. Did she even realise that? He should have escorted her down, he thought again. But the lady, and everything about her body language, had said a very definite no.

Shaking off the lusty thoughts, he rolled down his shirtsleeves. Damn Earl, the SOB who'd fathered him, for dying and leaving him this mess to sort out. No one knew of Jake's connection to this club, with the exception of Ry and his parents and more recently his PA.

And now Emma Byrne.

'Hell.' He checked the time, then shoved his phone in his pocket. He didn't have time for that particular complication right now—he had an important business meeting to attend. Grabbing his jacket from the back of his chair, he headed downstairs.

CHAPTER TWO

AND she'd told him not to turn up late.

'She'd better have a good excuse,' Jake muttered the following evening as he swung a left in his BMW and headed for Sydney's seaside suburb of Coogee Beach, where Emma lived with her mother and Stella. As Ryan's best man he'd had no choice but to elect himself to conduct the search party.

Or maybe she'd decided she didn't want to run into Jake Carmody again so soon.

She'd always been big on responsibility, he recalled, and tonight was her sister's night, so he figured she wouldn't opt out without a valid reason. But she hadn't answered her mobile and concern gnawed at his impatience. He tapped the steering wheel while he waited at a red light. A trio of teenagers skimpily dressed for a night on the town crossed in front of him, their feminine voices shrill and excited.

Maybe Emma wasn't the same girl these days. Maybe she had decided to swap those self-imposed obligations for some fun at last. After all, apart from those few minutes yesterday, when neither of them had actually been themselves, how long had it been since he'd seen her?

His gut tensed an instant at the memory. He knew exactly when he'd last seen her. Seven months ago at Stella and Ryan's engagement party. He knew exactly what she'd

been wearing too—a long, slinky strapless thing the colour of moon-drenched sea at midnight.

Or some such garment. He forced his hands to loosen
on the wheel. Unclenched his jaw. So what if he'd noticed
every detail, down to the last shimmering toenail? A guy
could look.

He'd arrived in time to see her leave hand in hand with
some muscled blond surfie type. Wayne something or
other, Stella had told him. Apparently Emma and Wayne
were a hot item.

Maybe Surfer Boy was the reason she'd lost track of
time...

Frowning at the thought, he pulled into the Byrnes'
driveway overlooking the darkening ocean. The gates were
open and he came to a stop beside an old red hatchback
parked at the top of a flight of stone steps.

Perched halfway down the sloping family property was
the old music studio, where he remembered spending af-
ternoons in the latter days of high school. Early-evening
shadows shrouded the brick walls but muted amber light
shone through the window. Emma lived there now, he'd
been informed, and she was obviously still at home. In the
absence of any other car on the grounds, it seemed she was
also alone.

Swinging his car door open, he pulled out his phone.
'Ry? Looks like she hasn't even left yet.' He strode to the
steps, flicking impatient fingers against his thigh. 'We'll
be there soon.'

Pocketing the phone, he continued down the stairs. If
he could make it on time to this wedding dinner after the
hellish day he'd had, trying to stay on top of two busi-
nesses, so could Emma. She was the bridesmaid, after all.

Some sort of relaxation music drifted from the window,
accompanying the muted *shoosh-boom* of the breakers on

the beach. He slowed his steps, breathing in the calming fragrant salt air and honeysuckle, and ordered himself to simmer down.

The peal of the door chime accompanied by a sharp rapping on her front door jerked Emma from her work. She refocused, feeling as if she was coming out of a deep-sleep cave. She checked her watch. Blinked. *Oh, no.* She'd assured Stella she'd be right along when the family had left nearly half an hour ago.

Which officially made her the World's Worst Bridesmaid.

She stretched muscles cramped from being in one position too long and assured herself her lapse *wasn't* because her subconscious mind was telling her she didn't want to see Jake. She would *not* let him and that crazy moment yesterday when their eyes had met and the whole world seemed to fade into nothing affect her life. In any way.

Rap, rap, rap.

'Okay, okay,' she murmured. She slipped the order of tiny stacked soap flowers she'd been wrapping back into its container and called, 'Coming!'

Running her hands down the sides of her oversized lab coat, she hurried to the door, swung it open. 'I...'

The man's super-sized silhouette filled the doorway, blocking what was left of the twilight and obscuring his features, but she knew instantly who he was by the way her heart bounded up into her throat.

'Jake.' She felt breathless, as if she'd just scaled the Harbour Bridge. Ridiculous. Scowling, she flicked on the foyer light. She tried not to admire the view, she really did, but her eyes ate up his dark good-looks like a woman too long on a blond boy diet.

Tonight he wore tailored dark trousers and a chocolate-coloured shirt open at the neck. Hair the colour of aged whisky lifted ever so slightly in the salty breeze.

'So here you are.' His tone was brusque, those black-coffee eyes focused sharply on hers.

'Yes, here I am,' she said, trying to ignore the hot flush seeing him had brought on and reminding herself where she'd seen him last. The flashback to the strip club made her feel like a gauche schoolgirl and it should not. But she was the one at fault tonight—and the reason he was standing in her doorway.

She gave him a careless smile, determined not to let yesterday spoil this evening. For Stella's sake. 'And running late,' she rushed on. 'I assume that's why you're here?' *Why else?*

One eyebrow rose and she knew he wasn't impressed. 'You had some people concerned.' He said it as if he didn't count himself amongst those people—where had yesterday's twinkle gone?—while he stepped inside and scanned the dining room table covered in the hand-made goat's milk soaps she'd been working on.

'You weren't answering your phone.' His gaze swung back to hers again. 'Not handy when people are trying to contact you.'

Her smile dropped to her feet. Was that *censure* in his voice? 'This from the guy who was too busy at his *other business* to answer his own mobile yesterday?' she shot back. 'You do realise I had to pry the info as to your whereabouts from your PA?'

He nodded, his eyes not flinching from hers. 'So she told me. I apologise for the inconvenience, and for any embarrassment I caused you.'

Emma drew in a deep breath. 'Okay.' She forced her mature self to put yesterday's incident to the back of her mind for now. 'As for me, I have no legitimate excuse for forgetting the time, so it's my turn to apologise that you had to be the one to come and get me.' She tried a smile.

He nodded, his dark eyes warmed, and his whole demeanour mellowed like a languid Sunday afternoon. 'Apology accepted.' He leaned down and brushed her cheek with firm lips, and she caught a whiff of subtle yet sexy aftershave before he straightened up again.

Whoa. Yesterday's tingle was back with a vengeance, running through her entire system at double the voltage. 'So...um...I'll just go...' Feeling off-centre, she backed away, ostensibly towards the tiny area sectioned off by a curtain which she used as a bedroom, but he didn't take the hint and leave. 'Look, you go on ahead. I'll be ready in a jiff and it's only a ten-minute drive to the restaurant.'

He shrugged, stuck his hands in his trouser pockets. 'I'm here now.'

Slipping off her flats, she glanced about for her heels. But her eyes seemed drawn to him as if they were on strings. He dressed like a million bucks these days. Still, those threadbare jeans he'd worn way back when had fuelled more teenage fantasies than she cared to remember. She watched him wander towards her table of supplies. With his hands in his pockets, drawing his trousers tight across that firm, cute butt...

No. Sleazy club-owner. Dragging her eyes away, she scoured the floor for her shoes. 'There's really no need to wait...'

'I'm waiting. End of story.' She heard the crinkle of cellophane as he examined her orders. 'Your hobby's still making you some pocket money, then?'

Irritation stiffened her shoulders. She glared at him. 'It's *not* just a hobby, and it's never been about the money.' *Unlike others who shall remain Nameless.* Exhaling sharply through her nose, she swiped up a black stiletto and slipped it on. 'I have to wonder why it is that helping people with skin allergies seems to you to be a waste of time.'

'I never sa—'

'Why don't you go while I...?' *Calm down.* 'Find my other shoe.'

'So uptight.' He tsked. 'You really need to get out more, Em. Always was too much work and not enough play with you.' He scooped her shoe from beneath a chair and tossed it to her. 'Maybe the wedding'll help things along.'

She caught it one-handed, dropped it in front of her with a clatter and stepped into it, then bent to do up the straps. She'd had it with people telling her how to live her life. Get out more? She let out a huff. She had familial obligations. Had she told him what she thought of the way he was living *his* life nowadays? No.

She finished fastening her shoes and straightened, pushed at the hair that had fallen over her eyes. Forget his uninformed opinion. Forget him, period. She had her *un*-fabulous job at the insurance call centre—but it paid the bills—and she had just finished her Diploma in Natural Health. And if she chose to fill her leisure hours working on ways to help people use natural products rather than the dangerous chemicals contained in other products these days, it was nobody's business but hers.

'So how's...what was her name...? Sherry?' she asked with enough sweetness to decay several teeth as she slipped open the top button of her lab coat. 'Will she be missing you this evening?'

His brows rose. 'Who?'

'The one...' *draped all over you* '...at Stella's engagement party. Stella mentioned her name,' she hurried on, in case he thought she'd actually asked. Which she had. But he didn't need to know that.

'Ah...You mean Brandy.'

She shrugged. 'Brandy. Sherry. She looked like more of a *Candy* to me.' With her suck-my-face-off lips and over-generous cleavage. And everything else Emma was lacking. 'You didn't say hello and introduce us. Was that because she was one of your *exotic dancers?*'

'You and your date left as we arrived. Was that just a curious coincidence?'

Jake watched her cheeks flush guiltily and felt an instant stab of arousal. Hell. He kept his expression neutral, but something was happening here. And the hot little fantasy he'd had last night about what she'd been wearing beneath that red coat yesterday wasn't helping.

And now she was undoing the second button of that lab coat, revealing a pair of sexy collarbones and putting in-appropriate ideas into his head.

He ground his teeth together as images of black lace and feminine flesh flashed through his mind. 'Are you going to get ready or what?' The demand came out lower and rougher than he'd have liked. Then he held his breath as she shrugged out of the coat, tossed it over the couch.

'I'm ready already.' She flashed him a cool look. 'I use the coat to protect my clothes when I'm working.'

His gaze snagged on her outfit—a short black dress shot through with bronze, hugging her slender curves to perfection. He swallowed. The legs. How come he'd never noticed how long her legs were? How toned and tanned? He did *not* imagine how they'd feel locked around his waist.

Cool it. He deliberately relaxed tense muscles. He'd wait outside, get some air.

But before he could move she picked up an embroidered purse from the couch and walked to the front door. 'Shall we go?'

He walked ahead, opened the door. 'We'll take my car.'

'I'm taking my own car, thanks.' She locked the door behind them, then headed towards the hatchback, her heels tapping a fast rhythm on the concrete.

He pressed his remote and the locks clicked open. 'Hard to get a parking space anywhere this time of night,' he advised. 'And we—make that *you*—are running late already. Stella and Ryan are waiting.'

Swinging her door open, she glanced back at him. 'Better get a move on, then.'

He started to go after her, then changed his mind. She was in a dangerous mood, and he was just riled enough to take her on. And it might end… He didn't want to think about how it might end. Because he had a feeling that anything with Emma would need to be very slow and very, *very* thorough. If you could find your way through those thorns, that was. 'I'll see you there.'

She clicked her seat belt on, turned the ignition and revved the engine. 'Ten minutes.'

Emma's stomach jittered. Her pulse raced. Trouble. She'd seen more than enough of it in Jake's hot brown eyes. As if she was performing some sort of striptease. She'd not given it a thought when she'd peeled off her lab coat. But he had. *Sheesh.* She scoffed to herself. As if he'd give her less than average body a second look when he was surrounded by all those Brandies and Candies and brazen beauties at the Pink Mango.

Flicking a glance at her rearview mirror she caught the glare of his headlights. She deliberately slowed her speed, hoping he'd overtake, but he seemed content—or irritated enough—to cruise along behind her. She could feel his eyes boring into the back of her head.

She let out a shaky sigh and drew a deep, slow breath to steady herself. Easier to blame him than to admit to that old attraction—because no way was Jake the Rake the kind of man she wanted to get involved with on an intimate level.

She accelerated recklessly through a yellow light, Jake hot on her heels. She wasn't herself tonight. Wrong. She hadn't been herself since she'd come face to face with Jake in his dingy office yesterday.

Even as a teenager he'd always made her feel...different. Self-conscious. Tingly. Uncomfortably aware of her feminine bits.

Her fingers clenched tighter on the steering wheel. She needed to get herself under control. She didn't figure in his life at all, nor he in hers. And tonight wasn't about her or him or even *them*; it was about Stella and Ryan.

She tensed as the well-lit upscale restaurant came into view, and glanced in the mirror again just in time to see Jake's car glide into a parking space she'd been too distracted to notice right outside the restaurant.

Oh, for heaven's sake, this was ridiculous. The restaurant was on a corner and she stopped at a red light, tapping impatient fingers on the dashboard. Seriously, if it wasn't Stella's night she'd turn around and go home, pull the covers over her head and not surface till Christmas—

The thump on the car's roof nearly had her foot slipping off the brake as Jake climbed in beside her. 'Don't you know better than to leave your passenger door unlocked when you're driving alone at night?'

She hated his smug look and lazy tone and looked away quickly. 'Don't you know better than to scare a person half to death when they're behind the wheel?'

'Light's green.'

She clenched her teeth, pretending that she hadn't noticed his woodsy aftershave wafting towards her, and crossed the intersection. 'What are you doing here? There's no sense in both of us being late.' She saw a car pulling out ahead, remembered at the last second to check her rear vision and slammed on the brakes.

'We'll walk in together, *Scarlett.*'

'Don't remind me,' she muttered. She slid the car into the parking spot, yanked the key from the ignition, jumped out and locked her door before he'd even undone his seat belt.

Jake took his time getting out, watching her walk around the car's bonnet to the footpath. Not looking at him. No trace of the blue-eyed poppy tonight, he thought, locking his own door. She was as prickly as a blackberry bush.

The pedestrian light turned green. She left the kerb and he fell into step beside her. 'If we're going to pull this wedding business off, we need to be seen to be getting along.'

She jerked to a stop outside the restaurant. 'Fine.'

Catching her by her slender shoulders, he turned her to face him, noticed her stiffen at the skin-on-skin contact. 'We'll need to have a conversation about that at some point.'

'There's nothing to talk about.'

Light from the window spilled over her face. Wide eyes stared up at him, violet in the yellow glow. He slid his hands down her bare arms, felt her shiver beneath his palms and raised a brow. 'Nothing?'

'Nothing.' She rubbed her palms together, her gaze flicking away. 'It's chilly. I should've brought a jacket. I left it on the bed...'

No, he thought, she'd been distracted. Grinning, he let her go. 'Lighten up, Em, and give yourself permission to enjoy an evening out for once.'

CHAPTER THREE

WITH a light hand at her back, Jake ushered Emma into the upstairs restaurant. Exotic Eastern tapestries lined the burgundy walls. On the far side, through double glass doors was a narrow balcony crowded with palms. Dreamy Eastern music played softly in the background. The tempting aromas of Indian cuisine greeted them as they made their way towards the round family table already covered in a variety of spicy smelling dishes.

'Apologies, everyone.' Jake nodded to the happy couple. 'Glad to see you've already started.'

Emma murmured her own apologies to Stella while Ryan spooned rice into two empty bowls and passed them across the table. 'We wondered whether you two had decided to play hooky.'

'We thought about it—didn't we, Em?' Jake grinned, enjoying her appalled expression, then turned to Ryan's father.

Gil Clifton, a stocky man with wiry red hair and always a genuine smile, rose and shook hands. 'Good to see you again, Jake.'

'And you. We must get around to that tennis match.'

'Any time. Just give us a call and drop by.'

'I'll do that.'

Gil's smile faded. 'I was sorry to hear about your father. If there's anything I can do...'

The mention of the old man left nothing but a bitter taste in Jake's mouth and an emptiness in his soul that he'd come to terms with years ago. As far as he was concerned Gil and Julie Clifton were the only adult support he'd ever needed. 'Got it covered, thanks, Gil.'

He kissed Julie's cheek. 'How's the mother of the groom holding up?'

'Getting excited. And, to echo Gil's words, if you want to drop by and chat...you're always welcome.'

If Jake was ever to be lost for words now was that time. Ryan's family were the only people who knew about his dysfunctional childhood, and now the whole table knew about Earl. He forced a smile. 'Thanks.'

Emma watched Julie give Jake's arm a sympathetic squeeze. It occurred to her how little she really knew of his background beyond the fact he was Ryan's mate.

'So how's business?' Gil asked as Jake moved to the two empty chairs.

'Busy as usual. Evening, Bernice.'

'Jake.' Emma's mother acknowledged him coolly, then turned the same stony gaze on Emma. 'Thank you for collecting my unpunctual daughter.'

Emma reminded herself she was Teflon coated where her mother's barbs were concerned. The others resumed their conversations while she took the empty seat that Jake pulled out beside her mother and whispered, 'Sorry, Mum.'

'Have to admire our Emma's work ethic, though,' Jake remarked as he sat down beside her. 'It's not easy juggling two jobs.'

'Two jobs?' Bernice bit off the words. 'When one's a waste of time, I—'

'Mum.' Emma counted to ten while she reached for her

table napkin and smoothed it over her lap. 'How are you enjoying the food?'

Bernice stabbed at a cherry tomato on her plate. 'You need two *proper* jobs to be able to afford a dress like that.'

Jake smiled at Bernice on Emma's other side. 'And it's worth every cent. She looks sensational, don't you think? Wine, Em?'

'No, thank you. Driving.' She acknowledged Jake's support with a quick nod and reached for the glass of water in front of her. She took several swallows to compose herself before she said, 'I bought it at Second Hand Rose, Mum. That little recycle boutique on the esplanade.'

When her mother didn't reply, Emma turned to Jake. 'I didn't know about your father,' she murmured as other conversation flowed around the table. 'I'm sorry.'

He didn't look at her. 'Don't be.' He tossed back his drink, set his glass on the table with a firm *thunk* and turned his attention to something Ryan was saying on his other side.

Ouch. Emma reached for the nearest dish, a mixed vegetable curry, and ladled some onto her plate. He didn't want to talk about his father—fine. But there was a mountain of pain and anger there, and… She paused, spoon in mid-air. *And what, Emma?*

He clearly wasn't going to talk about it. He didn't *want* to talk about it—not with her at any rate—and she had no business pursuing it. It wasn't as if they were close or anything.

A moment later Jake turned to her again. 'I was abrupt. I shouldn't have been.'

An apology. Of sorts. 'It must be a tough time, no matter how you and he…' The right words eluded her so she reached for the nearest platter instead. 'Samosa?'

'Thanks.' He took one, put it on the side of his plate.

'I've been thinking about you, Emma.' He leaned ever so slightly her way, with a hint of seduction in the return of that suave tone.

She could feel the heat bleed into her cheeks. 'I don't—'

'Have you considered selling your supplies over the internet?' He broke off a piece of naan bread. 'Could be a profitable business for you. You never know—you might be able to give up your day job eventually.'

'I don't want to give up my day job.' *I'm not a risk-taker. Mum depends on me financially. I can't afford to fail.*

'I could help you with your business plan,' he continued, as if she'd never spoken. He lowered that sexy voice. 'You only have to ask.'

His silky words wrapped around her like a gloved hand and an exquisite shiver scuttled down her spine. She could imagine asking him…lots of things. She wondered if his sudden interest and diversionary tactics had anything to do with taking the focus off his own family problems. 'I don't have time to waste on the computer, and I told you already it's not about the money.' *Business plan? What business plan?*

'Lacking computer confidence isn't something to be embarrassed about.'

'I'm n—' With a roll of her eyes she decided her protest was wasted—men like Jake were always right—and topped up her curry with a broccoli floret. 'I'm flat out supplying the local stores. I don't need to be online.'

'It would make it easier. And if your products are so popular why wouldn't you want to see where they take you?'

She would—oh, she *so* would. Her little cottage business was her passion, but technology was so not her; she wouldn't know where to start with a website, and her meagre income—which went straight into the household budget—didn't allow her to gamble on such a luxury. 'As I said, there's no time.'

'Maybe you need to change your priorities. Or maybe you're afraid to take that chance?' He eyed her astutely as he broke off more bread. 'The offer's always open if you change your mind.'

Was she so easy to read? An hour or so with Jake and he saw it already. Her fear of failure. Of taking that step into the unknown. He was the last person she'd be going to for help; she felt vulnerable enough around him as it was. 'Thank you, I'll keep it in mind.'

Over the next hour the meal was punctuated with great food, toasts to the bride and groom, speeches and recollections of fond memories.

Jake watched on, feeling oddly detached from the whole family and the getting-married scenario. What motivated sane, rational people to chain themselves to another human being for the term of their natural lives? In the end someone always ended up abandoning the other, along with any kids unlucky enough to be caught up in it.

Then Emma excused herself to go to the ladies' room and Julie claimed Bernice's attention with wedding talk. He breathed a sigh of relief that for now he wasn't included in the conversation.

A moment later he saw Emma on her way back and watched, admiring her svelte figure and the way her hips undulated as she walked. Nice. Last night's fantasy flashed back and a punch of lust ricocheted through his body. She'd been fire and ice yesterday at the club, and he couldn't help wondering how it might translate to the bedroom.

He saw her come to an abrupt halt as a newly arrived couple cut across her path. His eyes narrowed. Wasn't that...? Yep. Wayne whoever-he-was. Jake watched on with interest as Wayne's dinner partner hugged his arm a moment then walked to the ladies', leaving Emma and Surfer Boy facing each other.

More like facing off, Jake thought, studying their body language. Even from a distance he could see that Emma's eyes had widened, that her face had gone pale and that Surfer Boy was trying to talk himself out of a sticky situation fast. Emma spoke through tight lips and shook her head. Then, turning abruptly, she headed straight for the balcony.

Uh-oh, he thought, *trouble in paradise?*

Emma's whole body burned with embarrassment as she hurried for the nearest sanctuary. She pushed blindly through the glass doors and took in a deep gulp of the cooler air.

He'd had the nerve to introduce the girl. *His fiancée.* Rani—a dusky beauty, heavy on the gold jewellery—had flashed a brand-new sparkle on the third finger of her left hand and said they'd been seeing each other for *over a year.*

While Emma and Wayne had been seeing each other. *Sleeping* with each other.

The bastard.

He'd broken it off with Emma only a month ago. Said it wasn't working for him. No mention then of a fiancée. Obviously this Rani girl had what it took to keep a man interested.

The worst part was that Emma had let her guard down with him. She'd done what she'd sworn she'd never do— she'd fallen for him big time.

Shielded by palm fronds, she leaned over the railing and stared at the traffic below. But she wasn't seeing it—she was too busy trying to patch up the barely healed scars

and a bunch of black emotions, like her own stupid gull-
ibility. She'd been used. Deceived. Lied to—

'Emma.'

She jumped at the sound of Jake's voice behind her.
Embarrassment fired up again. He must have seen the
exchange. No point pretending it hadn't happened. 'Hi.'
She ran a palm frond through her stiff fingers. 'I was just
talking to an ex.'

'A recent ex, by the look of things.' Warm hands cupped
her shoulders and turned her towards him. He lifted her
chin with a finger, and his eyes told her he knew a lot more
than she wanted him to. 'Should I be sorry?'

She shook her head. 'I'm not very good company right
now.' Shrugging off the intimacy of his touch, she looked
down at the street again, at the neon signs that lit the restaurants and cafés.

'You didn't answer the question, Em,' he said softly.
'But, if you ask me, I'd say he's not worth being sorry over.'

'Damn right, he's not. That was his *fiancée.* According
to her, they've been together over a year.'

'Hmm. I see.'

'Unfortunately for me, I didn't.' She stared at the street.
'We were both busy with work and after-hours com-
mitments, but we always spent Friday nights together.'
Frowning, she murmured, 'I wonder how he explained
that to her?'

'Friday nights?' There was a beat of silence, then he
asked, 'You had, like, a regular slot for him, then?'

She watched a couple strolling arm in arm below them
and felt an acute pang of loss. 'We had an understanding.'

'He *understood* that you scheduled him into your working life like some sort of beauty session?'

Her skin prickled. Wayne had actually been the one
doing the *scheduling,* and Emma had been so head over

heels, so desperate to be with him, she'd gone along with whatever he'd asked. 'He had a busy schedule too.' Obviously. 'But Friday night was ours. And he was cheating all along.'

Why the hell was she telling Jake this? Of all people. She turned to him, dragged up a half-smile from somewhere. 'I'm fine. I was over it weeks ago.'

'That's the way.' He smiled, all easy sympathy, and gave her hand a quick pat. 'The trick is not to take these things too seriously.'

These things? Being in love was just one of *these things?* 'And you'd be the expert at that particular trick, wouldn't you?' She and Wayne had had an understanding. He'd betrayed her and *that was serious.*

To her surprise, he spoke sharply. 'Contrary to what you may think, I don't cheat.'

'Because you're not with a woman long enough.' As if *she* would know his modus operandi these days…she wasn't exactly a social butterfly. She looked up and met Jake's eyes—dark, intense, like Turkish coffee. 'Sorry.' She shrugged. 'It's just that you're here, you're male, and right now I want to punch something. Or someone.' Her gaze flicked down to the street. 'Nothing personal.'

He shoved his hands in his pockets. 'Emma, yesterday—'

'You live your way, I live mine.' She waved him off. 'We're not teenagers any more.'

But was she living her life her way? she wondered as she paced past the balcony's foliage and back. Or was she living for other people?

After her father had died, leaving them virtually penniless, Emma had spent years working menial jobs after school so that they wouldn't have to sell her maternal grandmother's home, and then had supported herself through her studies. Her mother had been diagnosed with clinical depression soon after their father's death, and Stella had taken on the role of main carer, but Emma had been the one with the ultimate financial responsibility.

She didn't mind giving up her time or her money, but her mother was recovered now and Emma's sacrifices went unacknowledged and unappreciated.

And now she'd discovered the man she'd loved had been cheating on her for God knew how long, and in Jake's opinion it was because she was so focused on her work.

But Jake knew nothing about it, and she intended for it to stay that way. It did *not* excuse Wayne. Even the fact that the girl was more exotic than she was, more voluptuous... more everything...was no excuse. She was tempted to run downstairs and tell him what she thought of him, let Rani in on his dirty little secret—except she never wanted to see him again and she'd only make herself look like a fool. 'If nothing else, I expect honesty in a relationship.'

'You call a regular Friday night bonk a *relationship?*' he said.

She met his stare with a defiant stare of her own. 'It suited us.'

'It suited *you.*'

She bit her lip to stop unwanted words from spilling out. 'I thought what we had was what he wanted too.'

'Yeah, I'm sure it was.'

His dry comment riled her further. She rubbed the chill from her arms while inside her the anger and hurt and humiliation burned bright and strong. Better him thinking she was an idiot than knowing the embarrassing truth— that she was a naïve, gullible idiot.

'Sometimes I get so damn tired of doing what everyone else wants. What other people expect...' She trailed off when she saw Wayne and Rani outside an Italian restaurant on the street below. While his *fiancée* studied the menu in the window he glanced up and met Emma's eyes.

Renewed outrage surged through the other emotions in a dark wave. She refused to step back, refused to be the one to break eye contact. How dared he? Their weekly love-in had been a lie. They'd been seeing each other for months and the whole time he'd been deceiving her.

Making a fool of her.

In an uncharacteristic move, she made a rude hand gesture…and it felt good. Especially when Wayne looked away first. She spun away towards Jake, finding an oddly reassuring comfort in his presence. 'And sometimes I just want to live my own life and to hell with everything and everyone.'

'So start now, Em,' he said, his voice gentle yet firm. 'Change your life. Do what you want for a change.'

She stared into those dark eyes holding hers. What *did* she want?

All she saw was Jake.

Every rational thought flew away. Every drop of sense drained out of her as she stepped nearer to him, her eyes only leaving his to drift to his mouth.

What I want…

Before she could warn herself that this was a Really Bad Idea, she launched forward, cupped his jaw between her hands and plastered her lips to his.

Her heart gave a single hard jolt, and a little voice whispered, *This is what I've been waiting for.* The sizzle zapped all the way to her toes and back again before frustration and fury liquefied into heat and hunger. She flung herself into the moment, indulging her senses. The warmth of his mouth against hers was a counterfoil for his cool, refreshing scent—like moss on a pristine forest floor.

Caught off guard, Jake rocked back on his heels before

steadying himself, and her, his hands finding purchase on the smooth slope of her hips as he kissed her back.

Emma. Her taste—new and unforgettably sweet. The fragrance of soap and shampoo and woman all wrapped up in the texture of skin-warmed silk beneath his fingers.

She was a rising tornado of emotion and needs, and it whipped around the edges of his own darker desires. The word *complication* lurked somewhere at the back of his mind. He shrugged it away and instead, sliding his palms around to her back, hauled her closer and settled in to savour more of the exquisite sensations battering him.

'Ohh…' The sound was exhaled on a strangled gasp as firm hands pushed at his chest. She jerked out of his hold, eyes wide. 'I didn't… That was…'

'Nice,' he finished for her. His hormone-ravished body protested the gross understatement even as he knew she was just using him to get back at the drivelling idiot probably still watching the performance from the other side of the street.

As quickly as it had blown in the whirlwind subsided leaving only a tantalising whisper as she stared up at him, rolled her lips between her teeth and said, 'I don't know why I…did that.'

'You were upset. I was here.' Enjoying the way her eyes reflected her conflict, he couldn't help but grin. 'Have to tell you it wins hands down over the punch you threatened to dole out earlier.'

'I…need to see if Mum's ready to go home.'

'Emma.' He lifted a hand, dropped it when she edged farther away. 'Don't beat yourself up. It was just a kiss. And I'm sure Wayne got the message.'

She flinched as if he'd hit her. '*He* wasn't the… He wasn't look— I was… Oh, forget it.'

And in the light filtering through from the restaurant

he glimpsed twin spots of colour flag her cheeks before she whirled around and made a dash to the door.

Shoving his hands into his pockets, he leaned a hip against the railing while he waited for his body's horny reaction to subside. *You kiss me like that, honey, I ain't gonna forget.*

It was too bad she'd come to her senses so quickly. He didn't mind being used when it came in the form of a beautiful woman in distress—particularly when the woman had seemed oblivious that she *had*, in fact, used him. He looked down at the street. No sign of the scumbag.

He could still smell Emma; the fresh, untainted fragrance lingered in the air, on his clothes. The flavour of that one luscious kiss still danced on his tastebuds. The surprise of it—of *her*—like the first green sprout emerging from the carnage of a bushfire, still vibrated along his bones. She'd reacted without thinking for a hot and heavy moment there, and he'd enjoyed every second.

So had she.

And he wasn't going to let her forget either. Her weekly love-in arrangement proved she did casual. And she expected honesty from her lover. They had something in common on both counts.

He watched her walk towards a group who were preparing to leave and smiled to himself. The upcoming wedding weekend was looking better and better.

Emma gulped in a calming breath, drew herself tall, and walked unsteadily towards her table, trying not to remember she'd just kissed Jake Carmody senseless. Correction: *she* was the one who was senseless. The dinner left-overs had been cleared away. Only a rumpled and food stained red tablecloth remained. And a few curious faces were aimed her way.

'Emma…' Stella trailed off, her gaze sliding over Emma's shoulder.

The back of Emma's neck warmed. Her cheeks scorched. 'Um…sorry.' Was it possible to speak more than one word at a time? She waved a hand in front of her face. 'Needed some air.'

'We were starting to wonder whether you two had slipped away without—'

'Jake and I were just catching up.' She collected her purse. 'Mum, are you ready to leave? I've got some work to do before I go to bed.' She didn't wait for an answer, moving around the table saying her goodnights.

'Can I get a lift with you?' Stella reached for her own bag. 'Ryan's taking his parents home, and I want a couple of early nights this week.'

'Sure.' Emma steered clear of Jake, muttering a quick goodnight without looking at him, and from a safe distance on the other side of the table, then headed for the stairs.

'You okay, Em?' Stella asked beside her as they drove home. 'You're awfully quiet.'

'Wayne came into the restaurant while we were there,' she said, her voice tightening. 'With his fiancée.'

'Oh. Oh, Em. I'm sorry. You guys split up—what?— only a month ago?'

'What did you expect?' her mother piped up from the back seat. 'If you mixed with the right people like your sister, instead of hiding away in that studio night after night, y—'

'I'm not hiding.' Emma sighed inwardly. Stella had nursed their mother, then fallen in love with a wealthy man; in Bernice Byrne's eyes her younger daughter could do no wrong. 'I enjoy what I do, Mum.'

'Like you enjoyed cleaning other people's toilets and

stocking supermarket shelves after school too, I remember. Just another excuse not to meet people.'

Emma pressed her lips together to stop the angry words from rushing out. *Yeah, Mum? Where would we be if I hadn't? In a rented bedsit on the wrong side of town. Not in Gran's home, that's for sure.*

'Mum, that's not fair.' Stella spoke sharply.

'It's not, Stella. But then, life's not always fair—right, Mum?' Emma glanced at her mother in the rearview mirror. 'And sometimes it makes us hurt and lash out and say things we shouldn't. So I forgive you. You're not sorry about Wayne, Stella, and neither am I. And I don't want to talk about it. *Him.*'

'No, you'd rather kiss that good-for-nothing Jake Carmody behind the palms like some floozie,' her mother muttered.

Emma jolted, her whole body burning with the memory. And her mother, of all people, had obviously seen the entire catastrophe. Something close to rebellion simmered inside her and made her say, 'Jake's hardly a good-for-nothing, Mum—he has a well-established practice in business law.' She couldn't help feeling a sense of indignation on his behalf.

The strip club aside, she knew enough about Jake to know he'd worked hard all those years ago, taking jobs where he could get them to pay his way through uni.

Whereas Ryan came from old money. He'd graduated in the sciences and held a PhD in Microbiology—all expenses paid by Daddy. Then he'd volunteered his skills in Africa for a couple of years before hooking up again with Stella.

From the corner of her eye she saw Stella shift in her seat and turn to look at her. Suddenly uncomfortable, Emma lifted a shoulder. 'What?'

'Jake *kissed* you?' she said slowly. 'Like a proper kiss?'

'Not exactly.' Emma couldn't resist a quick glance at her mum in the mirror again. 'Mum got it right. It was more like…I kissed him.' As she relived that moment something like exhilaration shot through her bloodstream. 'What about it?'

'Ooh, that's so…hmm… You and Jake?'

Emma heard the smile in her sister's voice, could almost hear her mind ticking over.

'Wouldn't it be cool if—?'

'*Not* me and Jake. You know him. Every red-blooded female in Sydney knows him. Didn't mean anything.'

'But—'

'No buts.'

'Okay. *But*… The wedding will give you two time to catch up. You liked him well enough when we were younger, I remember.'

'Yeah—in a galaxy far, far away.'

'Not that far, Em. He lives in Bondi now. Only an hour's stroll along the coast…if you feel inclined.'

'I don't. I won't.'

But she couldn't blot him from her mind when she crawled into bed that night. She *had* been looking forward to seeing Jake again, even if it was only to assure herself she was well and truly over him.

But she didn't want to catch up with a seedy strip club owner who used women for his own purposes—both for his personal satisfaction and his burgeoning bank account.

But, oh, that moment of insanity…his lips on hers, his hands tugging her against the heat of his hard, muscled body…

And it *was* insanity. She stared up at the music room's low stained ceiling and tried not to hear the thick elevated thud of her heartbeat in her ears. She could have kept it simple. A friendly few days in the company of a good-looking guy. But she'd kissed him like one of his Brandies or Candies...and she'd changed everything.

CHAPTER FOUR

STIFLING a yawn, Emma glanced at her watch and wondered if Stella's hen's party would ever end. Twelve-thirty. The male stripper had done his thing and left to raucous feminine laughter and a wildly improper proposition or two over half an hour ago. The girls were now sitting around Emma's table drinking what remained of a bottle of vodka.

Emma had sat on one glass of wine the entire evening. She needed a clear head. She still had half a dozen orders to fill when the others left.

Emma glanced at the bleary-eyed girls in various stages of intoxication as Joni poured the remains of the vodka into her glass and laid the bottle on its side on the table. 'Don't any of you girls have to work in the morning?' she asked.

'It's Friday tomorrow,' Joni said, spinning the bottle lazily between two fingers. 'Nothing gets done on a Friday anyway.'

'Well, I don't want to be a party pooper but I've got work to finish tonight.'

Karina pointed at her. 'You need to get a life, Emma Dilemma.' She downed her drink, slapped her glass on the table and slurred, 'Seriously. Your hormones must be shrivelling up with neglect. When was the last time you got laid?'

'Kar, give it a rest.' Stella shot Emma a concerned look. 'She broke up with her boyfriend a few weeks ago.'

Karina squinted at Emma through glazed green eyes. 'You had a *boyfriend?*'

Emma could see it in Karina's eyes—*How did you find the time?*—and her whole body tightened. 'He wasn't a boyfriend as such…' She picked up her glass, touched the rim against her lips. 'He was convenient. More like a bed buddy.' Even if Wayne *had* seen their relationship that way, in Emma's book bed buddies didn't cheat. When the gaggle of giggles subsided she angled her glass in Karina's direction. 'You'd be familiar with the concept of bed buddies.'

'Totally.' Karina grinned. 'Way to go, Em,' she enthused, then raised a hand. 'Okay, enough of the true confessions. We're hungry, aren't we, girls? And since you're the only sober one here, Emma Dilemma, how about being a good little bridesmaid and fetching us a burger from that shop down the road?'

'And fries,' Joni added, stuffing another chocolate in her mouth.

'I'll go to the drive-through. It's closer.'

Karina shook her head. 'Nuh-uh. We want real hamburgers with proper meat—not that cardboard stuff.'

'Yeah,' Joni agreed. 'With lashings of bacon.'

Stella leaned to the side and massaged Emma's neck a moment. 'Come on, Em. I *looove* you, sis,' she cajoled in a boozy voice, then pulled her purse from her bag. 'My treat.'

Emma pushed up. Anything for peace. 'Okay. Providing you take your orders and eat them somewhere else. I've got to work.'

'You're a good sport, Em.' Karina stood, slung an arm around Emma's neck. She patted Emma's backside, then grinned hugely. 'Off you go, now.'

* * *

'Told you they'd still be awake,' Ryan said as the limo pulled into the Byrnes' driveway.

They'd dropped off the rest of the guys from the bucks' night, but Ry had got it into his head to kiss Stella goodnight before going home, and Jake—well, he was along for the ride. It was his responsibility to ensure nothing happened to Ryan before the big day. It had nothing to do with Emma living here too.

'Not sure they'll appreciate us gatecrashing their evening.' With a few beers under his belt, Jake stretched his long legs out in front of him. He'd assured Stella he'd look out for Ryan, and he'd done a pretty good job. He glanced at the slightly worse-for-wear groom-to-be. Mostly. Then he looked down to the well-lit studio. 'What do you suppose the girls get up to on a hens' night?'

'We're about to find out.' Ryan was already fumbling with the door.

'Steady, mate. I promised Stella I'd get you home in one piece.'

'Whoa…' Ryan murmured as the limo's lights swept an arc across the driveway, whitewashing the unexpected view of a female figure half-in, half-out of a car. 'Nice arse.'

Jake blinked at the flash of leggings-clad backside poking out of the open door, then took his time to admire the slender thighs and shapely calves rising from a pair of silver stilettos. A spark of interest danced along his veins. 'Careful,' he murmured with a grin. 'You're practically a married man.'

'Doesn't mean I'm dead.'

But Jake's attention had focused on what looked like a neon sticker in the shape of a hand on the girl's backside. 'What *is* that?' He squinted. The words *Pat Me* glittered in gold. 'Don't mind if I do,' he murmured, still grinning. His grin faded. 'Isn't that Emma's car?'

'Reckon you're right.' Both men looked at each other. *'Emma?'*

They turned back to see her unfurling from the car's depths. Dropping a loose soda can into the carton on her hip, she righted herself only to freeze in the headlights like a stunned, lanky-legged gazelle.

Incredulous, Jake felt his whole body tense as he took in the view. *Hot.* Over the leggings she wore a slinky white sleeveless top with a scooped neckline, blanched in the glare and highlighting enough curves to start her own Grand Prix.

'Eyes off, buddy.' He cleared his suddenly dry throat. 'She's about to become your sister-in-law.'

But Jake wasn't honour-bound by any such restriction. Eyes still feasting on the mouthwatering sight, he unfolded himself and climbed out, leaning an elbow on the open door. Cool air hit him. He could smell burgers.

'Emma. Wow.'

He gave himself a mental kick up the backside. *Well said.* Spoken like a freaking teenager. Where the hell were his sophisticated, urbane conversational skills? But his brain didn't seem to be functioning because all his blood had drained below his belt.

She seemed to come out of her daze, eyes widening as they met his. 'You're not supposed to be here,' she said, tight-lipped, as she turned and headed for the door at a rate of knots.

'Careful...' he called. Too late—he was already moving forward as he saw her stiletto bend and her ankle crumple. He heard her swear before she landed on that watch-worthy rear end in front of him, the carton she'd been carrying landing beside her.

Ryan rescued the carton with a muffled, 'I'll get Stella,' and made his escape as Jake squatted beside her. 'Emma?' He reached for her elbows. 'Are you okay?'

Emma groaned, but not nearly as much from the pain shooting up her calf as from her spectacular fall from grace in front of *this* man. She felt Jake's hands on her, his warm breath washing over her face, and closed her eyes. 'Just let me die now.'

She heard that rich caramel chuckle of his. He had both her shoes off before she could stop him. Gentle fingers probed her ankle, and a voice laced with calm concern and a hint of amusement said, 'So this is what you girls get up to on hen nights. Ry and I were wondering.'

She started to shuffle away from him but felt her leggings snag on the rough cement. She heard a strange sound, like Velcro parting, and stopped abruptly. 'I'm okay,' she said, gritting her teeth. Or she would be if she didn't die of embarrassment first. 'Now go away.'

He moved around behind her, slid his hands beneath her arms and hauled her upright so that his body was in intimate contact with her back. His big, hot *masculine* body. Her practically naked back. And nothing but thin torn jersey between her bare bottom and his…pelvis. Liquid heat spurted into her cheeks, along her limbs and everywhere their bodies touched.

'I told you I'm fine.' She tried to shrug away from the intimate contact but he didn't budge.

'Test your weight on it,' he ordered.

Her ankle tweaked when she set it on the ground but she stifled a wince and said, 'See? Fine.'

'Yeah, I can see.'

Ryan and the girls spilled out of the studio just as Jake swept her up into his arms. In an automatic reaction she clutched at his shoulders, and for an instant of lunacy she wallowed in the strength and heat surrounding her.

Being held against Jake's chest and carried inside was like being lifted into the clouds. She gazed up at his square shadow-stubbled chin. And just above that were…those lips.

Instant tension gripped her insides and refused to let go. Had she so quickly forgotten she'd kissed those lips? And *how?* That she'd flung herself at this man in an instant of heightened emotion was going to have to live with the reminder for the rest of her life? Or until after the wedding at least.

'It's going to be okay, Stella, don't worry,' she told her sister as Jake set her on the saggy old couch. Right now she was more concerned with that ripping sound she'd heard. 'Pass me that sarong on the armchair, will you?'

'Are you chilled?' Stella said, her voice anxious. 'Do you want a blanket or something?'

'No—and stop hovering.'

Stella pulled the sarong off the chair. 'I'm not hovering.'

'Are too.' She grabbed the proffered garment. 'Thank you.'

'Um… Before I go, I should tell you that Karina…um…' She exchanged a look with Jake, who shook his head.

Emma darted a glance between the two of them. 'What?'

Stella let out a strangled sound behind her hand. 'Never mind.'

Squatting in front of Emma, Jake prodded her ankle and began issuing orders. 'Get rid of the girls, Stella. And then you might like to kiss your fiancé goodnight and send him on his way.'

Hearing their cue to leave in that no-nonsense masculine tone, the girls scuttled out with muffled giggles.

Panic rose up Emma's throat. 'No, stay, Stell. Let Jake go.' She glared at him, winding the sarong about her torso as high as possible under her arms. 'I bet he has a million things to do.'

He met Emma's eyes full-on for a few seconds, then studied her foot again. 'Some ice would be good here, Stella, before you go.'

Seconds later Stella produced a pack of frozen peas from Emma's fridge, handed it to Jake. 'I feel responsible...'

'Don't,' Emma said, tight-lipped. 'If these guys hadn't turned up everything would've been all right.'

'So this guy'll take care of it.' Easing the improvised cold pack around Emma's ankle, Jake waved her sister off. 'You have guests to see off and a fiancé to farewell. You've called the girls a taxi, right?'

Stella nodded.

'Okay, go to bed.'

'If you're sure...' Stella's eyes flicked between the two of them.

Emma couldn't decide whether there was a glint of something playful in her sister's baby blue eyes, but her voice was concerned enough when she said, 'Phone up to the house if you need anything, Em.'

Then she disappeared outside with the rest of the gang, leaving Emma alone with Jake. The voices faded and the bustling atmosphere disappeared, leaving a tension-fraught anticipation in the gaping stillness. So still that Emma could hear the nearby surf pounding the beach. The sound of her heart beating at a million miles an hour. Jake had to be able to hear it as well. Fantastic. She groaned inwardly. 'But you have to go too,' she told him. 'The limo...'

'I can call him back. He's booked and paid for till 3:00 a.m.' His voice lowered a notch. 'Unless you want me to stay longer?'

His head was bent over her foot so she couldn't see his eyes. Just the top of his glossy dark head and those impressive shoulders making the fabric of his sexy black shirt strain at the seams. Before she could tell him no, not on his life, he straightened.

'It doesn't seem to be swollen. You sure that's the only casualty?'

'Yes.' In his line of work he might see more than his fair quota of bare backsides, but he wasn't going to see hers. She squeezed her still smarting butt and trembling thighs tighter together. 'I can take care of myself.'

'It's not your cute *derrière* I'm interested in right now, Emma,' he said, and she wondered if she'd voiced her thoughts. *And what did he mean 'right now'?*

Her cheeks flamed and she pushed the frozen pack of peas away. 'I can walk.' Holding the edges of the sarong together, she rose, ignoring the glint of pain in her ankle, and took three tentative steps. 'See? Now I want to go to bed. I appreciate your concern, but I'd like it if you'd leave.'

He ignored her. 'You should rest it. You need to be fit for Saturday.' He picked her up again and moved swiftly across the room and past the privacy curtain. He set her on her bed, laid the peas against her ankle again, then placed his hands on either side of her lower legs. Looked into her eyes. 'And, remember, as best man I've got the first dance with you.'

He'd come to her rescue and allowed her to keep her dignity. And now he sounded so genuinely caring that a wry half-smile tugged at her mouth.

'With you to remind me I'm not likely to forget.' She had to admit it felt good to be pampered for once in her life, to have someone care enough to look out for her and not even remotely laugh at her embarrassment. She relaxed a little. 'Thank you. I feel like a kid again. All I need is the warm milk and honey.'

'Warm milk and honey?'

'Mum's panacea for everything. Rather, it used to be.' *Twenty years ago.*

Jake knew Emma had always been a keep-to-yourself kind of girl, whereas outgoing, fun-loving Stella had made friends easily. He knew, too, how Emma had changed when her father had died.

Leaning in, he watched her gorgeous eyes widen, smelled her soft feminine scent. 'No milk and honey, but this—' he touched his lips chastely to her forehead '—might help.'

He heard the barely-there hitch in her breath and drew back. His gaze dropped to her mouth and lingered. Unglossed but luscious. So tempting to lean down and... He felt his blood pressure spike. His good deed damn well wasn't helping *him*.

Don't. Her lips moved but no sound came out.

'Why not?' he murmured. 'You kissed me the other night and I can't return the favour?'

'That was...different.' Her voice was breathless and he got the impression she'd have pressed her rigid spine through the wall if she could.

'Yeah,' he said, recalling the firestorm which had engulfed them both for one unguarded moment. 'It was.'

'It was impulsive and selfish and I used you.'

Straightening up, he looked at her eyes, almost violet in the dim light from the single naked globe above the bed. 'I didn't mind. And, if we're being honest here, you didn't mind either.' He saw colour bleed into her cheeks and patted her leg. 'Take it from me, Surfer Boy wasn't right for you.'

'And you'd know that how…?' She stared at him out of soulful eyes. 'I sure as heck don't know Jake Carmody. You work in the sex industry.' Her voice rose with disapproval. 'You *own* that…that place. So you… It follows naturally that you're not ashamed to use and exploit women—often women with no other choices—to make money. And it's just *wrong,*' she went on. 'Does—?'

'I didn't buy the strip club. I inherited the place when Earl died.'

She frowned. 'Earl? Who's Earl?'

'My father.'

'Oh…' A slow exhalation of breath accompanied the word. She curled her fingers beneath her chin. 'So…your dad owned it.'

'Not "dad." That word implies some sort of familial bond and there wasn't any.' He refused to allow regret to intrude on his life. He didn't need family. He didn't need anyone. 'And before you say I should shut it down and walk away and there'd be one less sleazy club in King's Cross I have the staff to consider. I've found a potential buyer but we're negotiating; I want to ensure a fair deal for everyone.'

'Oh. Yes. Of course. I…' She trailed off, and maybe her eyes softened, but he couldn't be sure because for once in his life he wasn't really seeing the woman in front of him.

He scratched the niggling sensation at the back of his neck that he'd learned long ago to recognise as insecurity. He hadn't felt it in years. He made his own rules, controlled his circumstances, his life. Himself. Always.

Not this time.

He clenched his jaw against the feeling that the rules

had suddenly changed and his life was veering off course. And he might have left then but for Emma's soft voice.

'Your mother...is she...?'

'She lives in South America. She doesn't keep in touch.' After nearly two decades, her abandonment still had the power to slice at his heart. He'd always made a point of not getting personally involved in other people's lives because it would involve opening up his own.

'Do you have any siblings to help? Extended family?'

'No.'

'That must be tough for you, handling everything on your own.'

He shrugged dismissively. 'I'm a tough guy.' It was baggage he'd left behind years ago and he wasn't going there. Not for anyone.

She nodded slowly and smoothed the sarong over her legs. 'Look, I'm sorry if I sounded over the top, it's just that I have very firm thoughts about men who use women for their own purposes.'

He knew she was thinking of Surfer Boy. 'Acknowledged and understood.'

'Still, I am sorry about your dad...I can see it hurt you. If you wa—'

'Okay. Let's leave it at that.'

'So...um... How did it go with the guys' night?' She didn't seem in such a hurry to kick him out now, and he didn't know whether that was a good thing or not.

'Ry may need me to remind him tomorrow that he had a good time.'

'Did it include a visit to King's Cross by any chance?'

'Every bucks' night worth its mettle has to include a stop somewhere in King's Cross.' Unfortunately. He must be the only straight guy in Sydney who didn't find striptease a turn-on.

'Well, we girls enjoyed our own private stripper right here.' With a theatrical flick of her hair she drew her knees up to her chest, tucking the edges of the sarong beneath her feet.

'And how did that go?'

'Man, he was *hot*.' The instant the words were out her hands rushed to her cheeks. 'I've never seen a guy strip... well, not that way.' She sucked in her lips. Her cheeks were pink beneath her hands.

'Am I detecting a double standard here?' He couldn't resist teasing her. 'Okay for the girls to look but not the guys?'

'Oops!' Her pearl-tipped nails moved to her lips. 'Can I say I didn't look?'

'Afraid not.' He leaned closer. 'I have to tell you, you looked hot too, last night, in that sexy little number.'

Her smile, when it appeared, was a delight to behold. 'It *was* fun dressing up and feeling attractive for a change.'

'You should try it more often.'

'Try what?' Her smile disappeared. Her hands fell away from her face. A shadow flickered in her eyes—a blue moon sinking into an inky sea—as she crossed her arms and hugged her shoulders. 'Looking attractive? Gee, thanks heaps.'

'Fun, Emma. Just try having some fun.' He was barely aware that his hands had somehow moved towards her thighs, so close he could feel the heat from her body, and barely caught himself in time.

He jerked back and away. Pushed to his feet. If he stayed he was just un-sober enough to show her something about having fun...and he didn't want to think about the consequences if he did.

Not tonight.

'Since you don't seem to need me for anything, I'm

going to see if I can catch up with Ry after all. I haven't heard the limo leave yet.' He didn't know what demon prompted him to add, 'The night's still young. Might as well enjoy my evening off...'

He winked—he *never* winked—leaving Emma staring wide-eyed at him as he lifted a hand, then turned and walked away. ''Night.'

He let himself out and headed towards the limo at the top of the drive. He needed the brisk evening air to cool his groin. So much for keeping his past where it belonged. He'd moved on, made something of himself. Until Earl had died and all the old bad had rushed back.

He didn't need Emma messing with his head, trying to make everything all right. Maybe he should just keep things as they were. Acquaintances. Casual friends.

He came to an abrupt halt. Except...now he'd tasted her on his lips, enjoyed the slippery slide of her lithe womanly body against his. Seen and felt her respond as a woman did to a man she fancied...

Friends, *hell.* It was too late for that.

CHAPTER FIVE

'DID you ever see such a view?' Emma leaned over the balcony outside the room she was sharing with Stella for the night. 'You sure know how to pick a wedding venue. It's like some god has spread a knobbly green carpet over the Grand Canyon, then sprayed it with a fine indigo mist.'

'It helps that one of Ryan's uncles owns the place,' her sister said cheerily behind her.

Nestled on the edge of the escarpment at Echo Point, in the famous Blue Mountains west of Sydney, the exclusive boutique hotel was pure luxury. The majestic view of Jamieson Valley stretched out below them, equally breathtaking. As evening approached, soft golden light coloured the sky. Inky pools were swallowing up the valley floor, and the sun's last rays hammered the streaks of exposed rock with vermilion, carving deep purple shadows between.

Stella joined Emma at the balcony's wooden rail. 'The guys won't be seeing anything like this where they are.'

'No,' Emma murmured, drawing her tracksuit jacket closer as the air chilled. The guys and Ryan's parents were spending the night at a cosy little bed and breakfast in Katoomba, a two-minute drive away. 'But I'm sure they'll find something to entertain them.' Her tone was more caustic than she'd intended.

She was still brooding over the way Jake had swaggered out of the studio last night. She couldn't stop wondering what he'd got up to afterwards. Her fingers tightened on the cool wood. He'd *winked* at her. She knew exactly what he'd got up to.

And why on earth was she tying herself up in knots over it? It was precisely the kind of behaviour that reminded her that he had been, and obviously still was, a chick magnet. And why he was such a knee-buckling, sigh-worthy *experienced* kisser...

'So, Stella.' Forcing him from her thoughts, she linked arms with her sister and guided her back to the little glass table. 'Ryan can't wait for tomorrow. He's going to make a wonderful husband, and you're going to have lots of babies and live happily ever after, the way you always dreamed.'

She picked up their Cosmopolitan cocktails and offered a toast. 'To your last night as a single woman.'

As she sipped, Emma's gaze drifted inside, through the floor-to ceiling glass doors, to the two four-poster double beds with their embroidered snowy white covers and mountains of soft lace pillows.

Ryan's parents had footed the bill for the entire wedding and the wedding party's accommodation here tomorrow night. Ryan was their only child, and for them this extravagance was a drop in the ocean.

'You're marrying money, Stell. We might have been rich too if Dad hadn't made those bad investments just before he died.'

Stella nodded. 'Yeah, Mum never got over losing her inheritance that way.'

'She never got over *Dad*.' Even now their mother was in her own beautifully appointed room down the hall, alone. 'She let him destroy her,' Emma went on. 'Even beyond the grave she's still letting him colour her life grey.'

Emma reminded herself that she wanted no part of that pain. Wayne had temporarily clouded her vision with his good looks and smooth-talking charm, but now she saw everything through the crystal-clear lens of experience. No man would ever have that power over her again.

Stella set her glass down and touched Emma's hand. 'You've kept us together all these years with a roof over our heads and I want to thank you—'

'It was my responsibility as the elder sister to keep us safely off the streets.' She shook her head. 'You looked out for Mum—I had it easy compared to you. But I wanted a career too. All you ever wanted was to find the right man and get married.'

'Yeah.' Stella sighed. Then she smiled, her face aglow with a bride's radiance. 'But now I'm marrying Ryan I'll be in a position to help out. I've already decided—'

'Stella—'

'He and I have discussed it.'

'For Mum, then. Not for me.'

Stella met her eyes. 'You don't want to give away a bit of that independence and find someone to love and share your life with some day?'

'Love? No.' Because Stella's question had unsettled her, she cupped her suddenly cold hands beneath her armpits. 'I prefer lust. Less complicated.'

'You're hurting after what happened with Wayne,' her sister said gently, 'and that's okay because—'

'I told you last night. It was lust, not love.'

'Bed buddies?' Stella murmured, then shook her head. 'I don't believe you for one minute, Em. And I don't care what you say. You *do* want love somewhere down the track when you're over the love rat. I remember when we were kids and used to talk about the men we were going to marry. Your man had to own a house by the sea, he had to love animals, 'cos Mum refused to let us have pets and he had to own a cupcake shop.'

Emma smiled at her childish fantasies. 'What about your ivory castle?'

'We're staying in one in France.' Stella hugged her drink close to her chest. 'Not ivory, but a real medieval castle with its own resident ghost.'

Emma heard the signal for an incoming text and dug her phone out of her pocket to read the screen.

'How's the view where U R? J'

She frowned as a butterfly did a single loop in her stomach. She texted back: *'Glorious.'*

Setting the phone on the table, she reached for her drink and considered switching the thing off. She needed a clear head for tomorrow, and interacting with Jake beforehand—in any way, shape or form—wouldn't do her any favours.

A moment later another text appeared. *'Did U bring work?'*

She sipped her drink and looked at her phone a moment before answering: *'Yes.'*

Seemed he wasn't put off by her one-word texts, because the next one appeared a moment later.

'Not allowed. This weekend is about having fun.'

Fun and Jake...? A shiver tingled down her spine. He was a man who definitely knew how to have fun. She texted back: *'Is she a blonde?'*

'I have a certain brunette in mind. Meet me downstairs 4 a drink.'

The shiver spread to her limbs. *'Spending evening with sister. Remember her? 2moro's bride.'* She switched her phone off, shoved it back in her pocket.

'Who are you texting?'

'Jake.' She threw Stella an accusatory glance.

'Anything wrong?'

'He asked me to meet him for a drink.' She felt Stella's gaze and looked away, out over the darkening valley and the gold-rimmed purple clouds in the distance.

'Something you're not telling me, here?' Stella asked behind her.

'No.' She had the niggling feeling she was being set up by her sister.

'Jake likes women, but he's a good guy. Nothing like the love rat. He's not into commitment right now and, as you've clearly pointed out, neither are you...so are you going?'

'Of course not.' She turned around and met her sister's scrutiny full-on. Stella had a half-smile on her lips, as if she didn't quite believe her. Emma glared back. 'This is our last night together—you and me.' And she wanted to place some orders and research some alternative suppliers on her laptop at some stage.

'Well, I'm going to have a long soak in that to-die-for spa tub.' Stella rose, collected their glasses and walked towards the door. 'I won't miss you for an hour or so if you want to change your mind.'

'Nope.' Emma followed her in. 'I've got my music to keep me company.' So much for placing orders. Right now she couldn't remember a single item she needed, and music seemed a more soothing option.

The hotel's phone rang as Emma closed the balcony's glass doors and Stella stretched out on her bed to pick up. 'This is the bride's room,' she announced, with a bounce in her voice. 'You're speaking to the bride, who's just about to enjoy her own candlelit spa bath.' She grinned over at Emma, then rolled onto her back, listening to whoever was on the other end of the phone. 'Uh-huh. In the lobby. Ten minutes. Okay.'

Emma's pulse blipped. She sat on her own bed and unravelled her earphones. 'No.'

'But it's Ryan.' She hugged the phone to her chest. 'The guys had Chinese take-out and he has a fortune cookie for me—isn't that sweet of him?'

'It's not sweet, Stell, it's subterfuge.' Emma lay back and closed her eyes. 'Jake put him up to this, and I'll bet you your fortune cookie that it's Jake, not Ryan, down there.'

'Please, Em. You have to go to make sure. I can't see him now before the ceremony. It's bad luck.'

'And Ryan would *know* that.'

'*Pleeease?*'

'Fine,' she huffed, and sat up, clipping her iPod to her jacket.

'She said fine,' Stella told her caller, and hung up then grinned. 'Thanks, bridesmaid.'

Emma grabbed an elastic band from the nightstand and dragged her hair back into a tight ponytail. 'Only for you, and only because it's your wedding day tomorrow. Then I'm going for a run.'

'Take your time,' she heard Stella call as Emma let herself out of the room and headed for the stairs.

Jake disconnected with a satisfied grin. 'You don't need me for a while, do you, Ry? She said yes.'

Ryan was stretched out on the couch, checking out their honeymoon destination on his tablet PC but he glanced up as Jake pulled on a clean T-shirt. 'You're a sneaky devil.'

'Make that *smart* and sneaky.' He stuffed his wallet in his jeans. 'And your fiancée's as much to blame as me.'

'Then she's a sneaky devil too.' He tapped the screen. 'I don't know why I'm marrying her.'

Jake grinned and waggled his brows. 'Having second thoughts? It's not too late to back out, you know.'

'Ah, but the reception's paid for. Why waste good grog?'

'There's that.' His humour fading, Jake sat down on the end of the couch and studied his best mate. 'Seriously, Ry. Why the big commitment?'

Ry looked up, and Jake saw the furrows of concentration in his mate's brow smooth out and the corners of his mouth tip up. 'When you meet the woman you want to spend the rest of your life with you'll know why.'

'But *married?*' Jake mentally shuddered at the word. 'Why would you want to spend your life with one woman? Man wasn't meant to be monogamous.'

'Says who?'

'I read it in an article. Somewhere. A reputed scientific journal, if I remember right.'

'Okay, well, *this* man's monogamous.' Ry resumed tapping his screen.

'Maybe *now,*' Jake said. 'I remember when you and those twins—'

'Past history. I was at uni and Stell and I weren't seeing each other then.'

'But how do you *know* she's the one?'

Ry's finger paused. 'When I saw my children in her eyes I knew.'

Jake stared at the guy he'd thought he knew. 'Crikey, mate—break out the violins.'

Ry squinted at something on the screen, slid a finger over its surface. 'Just because you're not into the matrimonial thing doesn't mean others aren't.'

'Fair dinkum—*your children in her eyes?*'

Ry looked up, a lopsided grin on his face. 'Yeah. We want kids. A whole bunch of 'em.' His expression sobered. 'I guess the bottom line is I love Stella. For better or worse. I don't want to imagine my life without her.'

Jake didn't want to imagine a life without women either. But *one* woman for ever? Absolutely for worse. But a curious sensation gripped his chest, as if somehow Ryan had betrayed their friendship and left him standing on the outside looking in.

'So, are you going to tell me why you're playing sneaky devil?' Ry asked, his eyes focused on the screen once more.

Jake rose to hunt up the keycard for the room. 'Because the girl needs a kick up that seriously sexy backside—'

'Which I didn't notice, remember?'

'Yeah, I remember.' Something that might feel like possessiveness—if he were the type—clawed at the back of his neck. He didn't care for the sensation and rubbed it away, swiping the keycard from the bottom of his bed. 'She needs to come out of that shell she's been living in for the past however many years. There's more to life than work.'

Ry looked up, expression thoughtful. 'And you're going to be the one to show her? Careful. That's Emma you're talking about—she's not just any woman. And she's my future sister-in-law.'

'I'm aware of that,' he muttered, fighting the scowl that came from out of nowhere to lurk just beneath the surface of his skin. He planted a grin on his face and grabbed his jacket. 'Trust me.'

The moment the door shut behind him his smile dropped away, his own words echoing in his ears. Problem was, could he trust *himself*? But from the moment Emma Byrne had walked into the club in that sexy red coat, those blue eyes smoking and sparking with every challenge known to man, he'd not been able to think past getting her naked. He'd never intended acting on it—he liked his women without prickles, after all—but then there'd been that kiss at the restaurant... Sparks that hot demanded at least some sort of exploration.

He decided to walk the short distance to sample autumn's crisp mountain air. Cold. Bracing. Invigorating. Mind-numbing. Just what he needed. His breath puffed in front of him as he strode along Katoomba Street towards the girls' hotel.

After tomorrow it would never be the same between him and Ry again. He passed a warmly lit café, packed with Friday-evening diners, and hunched deeper into the warmth of his jacket. It reminded him that back in that room with Ry he'd felt...shut out. As if Ry was about to join a club Jake wasn't eligible for. Would never be eligible for.

Clenching his teeth against the chill, he crunched through a pile of autumn leaves, sending them scattering and twirling along the pavement in noisy abandon. He didn't want to join the matrimonial club.

Shut out.

His mother had shut him out of her life too. 'You look just like your father,' she'd accused her five-year-old son. Jake was reminded of that every time he looked in a mirror. She'd left her cheating husband and young look-alike child for a new life and a new marriage. Rejected him— her own flesh and blood.

And, yeah, he might be his father's spitting image— but had he inherited Earl's genes? He'd learned a lot about women in his formative years. After all, how many kids got to grow up in the back room of a strip club? With the smell of cheap perfume and sex in their cramped living arrangements. Falling asleep to carnal sounds through his tiny bedroom's paper-thin walls.

As a teenager blocking out those same sounds while trying to finish homework, because he'd known that to escape the place, to take control of his life and become a better man than his father, he needed to study.

Jake knew how to have a good time. A good time involved no strings, no stress. No emotion. Was he like his father in more ways than looks? He clenched his jaw as he turned a corner and the hotel came into view. *Shoot me now.*

He picked up his pace. Earl had used women, whereas Jake respected his partners. The women he associated with were professional career types more often than not—unlike Earl's. They were confident, intelligent and attractive, and they understood where he was coming from. He made it clear up front that he wasn't into any long-term commitment deals and they didn't expect more than he wanted to give.

It was honest, at least.

Emma was braced to see Jake, not Ryan, waiting in the lobby. So she took the three flights of stairs rather than the elevator. Deliberately slowly. Admiring the delicate crystal lighting along the hallway, the local landscape paintings on the walls as she reached the top of the ground floor. The thick black carpet emblazoned with the hotel's gold crest.

But seeing Jake standing at the base of the sweeping staircase as she descended, one bronzed hand on the newel post, dark hair gleaming beneath the magnificent black chandelier, with his jacket slung over his shoulder like some sort of designer-jeans-clad Rhett Butler...

Her hand was gliding along the silky wooden banister or her legs might have given out. She might even have sighed like Scarlett; she couldn't be sure. She was too busy shoring up her defences against those dark eyes and the heart-winning smile. Because she knew in that instant that this man could be the one with the power to undo her.

Slowing halfway down, she leaned a hip against the staircase, sucked in a badly needed breath. *Stay cool,* she told herself. *Cool and aloof and annoyed.* He thought he'd tricked her into coming but she knew better. Didn't she? She frowned to herself. She was here, after all.

Because Stella had asked her.

Right. Straightening, she resumed her descent, concentrating on not tripping over her feet, her eyes drawn to him no matter how hard she tried to look away. That sinner's smile and those darker-than-sin eyes…

'Are you feeling all right?' he asked when she reached the bottom step.

She looked at him warily. 'Why wouldn't I?'

'You looked as if you were swaying there for a second or two. I thought you were going to swoon, and then I'd have been forced to play the hero again.'

'I did not sway. Or swoon. And you are *not* my hero. I'm guessing there are no fortune cookies either.'

He grinned. 'You're guessing wrong.' He took her elbow, led her across the glittering marbled foyer. At intervals floor-to-ceiling glass columns illuminated from within threw up a clear white light. He stopped by a little coffee table with two cosy leather armchairs. 'Sit.'

She did, gratefully, sinking into the soft black leather.

He pulled two scraps of paper from his jeans pocket, checked them both, then placed one on her lap.

'This isn't a fortune cookie.'

'I have to admit Ry and I ate them. But we saved you girls the messages.'

She unrolled the little square. '"A caress is better than a career."' Where the heck had he found *that* little gem? 'Says who? *And* it would depend on who's doing the caressing.'

But her traitorous thoughts could imagine Jake's warm, wicked hands wandering over her bare skin… Lost in the fantasy for a pulse-pounding moment, she stared unsee-ingly at the paper in front of her. *For heaven's sake.*

She forced her head up, regarded him with serene in-difference. 'This isn't from a fortune cookie. You made these yourselves.'

He spread his hands on his thighs, all innocence. 'Why would I do that?'

'To get me downstairs, perhaps?'

His smile came out like sunshine on a cold day. 'You have to admit it's inventive.'

'Deceptive, more like.'

'Hey, Ry has to take some of the credit.'

She felt the smile twitch at the corner of her mouth. 'What does Stella's say?'

'"Two souls, one heart." Appropriately romantic, Ry thought.'

And Cool Hand Jake didn't, obviously. 'She'll prob-ably sleep with it under her pillow tonight.' Desperate to distance herself from his enticing woodsy scent and the thought of those coolly efficient hands on her heated body, she pulled her earphones out of her tracksuit pocket. 'Okay, now that's out of the way I'm off for a run.'

'Not so fast.' He reached over, circling her forearm in a loose grip. 'You're going to say you've got soap orders to type up or some such rubbish when you get back. Right?'

Right. If she could only remember what... The heat of his hand seemed to be blocking her ability to process simple thought. 'I—'

'To avoid me.'

She swallowed down a gasp. He was flying too close to the truth, and it threw her for a loop. 'Why would you matter th—?'

'You know it. I know it.' Cutting her off, he leaned forward, his hold tightening a fraction, his eyes boring into hers. 'Admit it.'

'Why?' Little spots of heat were breaking out all over her body.

'I matter to you.' He smiled—grinned, actually—teeth gleaming white in the light. 'How much do I matter, Emma?'

She pushed a hand over the crown of her head, her mind a jumble. 'Stop it. You're confusing me. This is the last evening I'll see my sister before she gets married. I…I'm going to spend the evening with her—a maid of honour thing.'

'Of course. And you can. In a little while.' His thumb abraded the inside of her wrist, sending tiny tingles scuttling up her arm. 'She won't mind,' he continued in that same liquid caramel tone. 'In fact I'm betting she's enjoying her soak in the spa right now.'

'It *was* you on the phone.'

'Guilty.' He grinned again, totally unrepentant. As if he pulled that kind of stunt all the time to bend women to his will. 'She's confiscated your laptop, by the way.'

'*What?*'

'Your sister agrees with me that you need time out from work.'

She gaped at him, incredulous. 'You two discussed my *needs?*' The image popped into her mind before she could call it back, along with the overly explicit, overly stressed word, and the whole calamity hung thick in the air like a sultry evening.

His eyes turned a warmer shade of dark. 'Not all of them. But we'll get to that. Stella wants you to enjoy her wedding, not be distracted by orders and schedules. She's concerned about you. And frankly—'

'What do you mean, "we'll get to that"? Get to what?'

Her voice rose on a crescendo. A couple of heads turned their way.

'This isn't the place,' he murmured, his voice all the quieter for her raised one.

Changing his grip, he pulled her up before she could mutter any sound of protest. He was so close she could feel the heat emanating from his body, could smell expensive leather jacket and freshly showered male skin.

'The place?' she echoed. 'Place for what?'

He entwined his fingers with hers. 'Why don't we take a walk and find out?'

CHAPTER SIX

EMMA blinked up at him through her eyelashes. It took her a scattered moment to realise she was still holding her earphones in her free hand and that her other hand was captured by the biggest, warmest hand it had ever come into contact with. She told herself she didn't want to be holding his hand...but who was she kidding but herself?

'*Run,*' she managed, pulling out of his grasp. 'I was going for a *run.*' And if she was sensible she'd keep running all the way back to Sydney.

'I'll join you.'

She glanced at his leather jacket and casual shoes, deliberately bypassing the interesting bits in between. 'You're hardly dressed for it.'

'I'll try to keep up.' *His* gaze cruised down her body like a slow boat on a meandering river, all the way to her well-worn sneakers. 'What about your ankle?'

'It's fine.' He'd be offering to carry her next, so she conceded defeat. 'Okay, we'll walk.' Stuffing her earphones back in her pocket, she accompanied him outside and onto the street.

The air had a cold bite and an invigorating eucalypt scent that called to her senses, and she breathed deep.

'I saw a little café on the way here,' he suggested.

'I didn't come to the mountains to be shut in a stuffy café with a bunch of city slickers up for the weekend.'

'Of which we're two,' he pointed out.

'I want to see the Three Sisters by night and sample some mountain air. Come on, it's a ten-minute walk to Echo Point.'

He took her hand again. 'What are we waiting for?'

They followed the hotel wall that enclosed the beautiful garden where tomorrow's ceremony would take place until it gave way to bushland fenced off from the road. Beyond, the ground fell away more than two hundred metres to the valley floor. Neither talked, but a feeling of camaraderie settled between them. Both were absorbed in the mutual appreciation of their surroundings.

The minute the famous Three Sisters rock formation came into view Emma came to an awed stop. 'Wow.' She hung back from the main vantage point where a few tourists were milling about, unwilling to share the moment with strangers.

Floodlit, the Sisters gleamed a rich gold against the black velvet backdrop, surrounding trees catching the light and providing a lacy emerald frame. The never-ending sky blazed with stars.

She sighed, drinking in the sight. 'Aren't you glad we didn't go for coffee?'

'That first glimpse always packs a punch, that's for sure.'

His voice rumbled through her body and she realised he'd let go of her hand while she'd been taking in the view and was now standing behind her, his chin on top of her head.

'Did you know the Aboriginal Dreaming story tells us there were three brothers who fell in love with three sisters from another tribe and were forbidden to marry?' She hugged her elbows, and it seemed natural to lean back into Jake's warmth.

In response, a pair of rock-solid arms slid around to the front of her waist. 'Go on. I'm sure there's more.'

'A battle ensued, and when the men tried to capture them, a tribal elder turned the maidens into stone to protect them.'

'And right there,' he drawled lazily, 'you're viewing a lesson to be heeded about the dangers of love and marriage.'

She turned within the circle of his arms. 'The sad thing is the sisters had no say in any of it.'

'But you do,' he murmured against her brow. And bent his head.

Warm breath caressed her skin and her heart began to pound in earnest. He was going to kiss her... And she wasn't in a fit state to be running anywhere.

Her legs trembled and her mind turned to mush as anticipation spun through her and she looked up. His face was so close she could feel the warmth of his skin, could see its evening shadow of stubble. He had the longest, darkest eyelashes she'd ever seen on a man. And his eyes... had she ever seen such eyes? As bottomless as the yawning chasm they'd come to view.

Then a half-moon slid from behind a cloud, bathing his perfect features in silver, as if the gods had hammered him so.

'You can tell me no.' He loosened his hold around her waist slightly. 'Right here in front of the Sisters you can exercise your free will as a modern woman. Push me away if you want. Or you can accept what we've been tiptoeing around for the past few days and kiss me.'

'Tiptoeing?' she whispered. 'I haven't—'

'And it's time it stopped.'

'Kiss you…?' Her words floated into the air on a little white puff as she looked up into his eyes. Dark and deep and direct. Had he mentioned free will? Her will had suddenly gone AWOL; she'd felt it drift out of her and hang somewhere over Jamieson Valley with the evening mist.

His gaze dropped to her mouth. Strong fingers curled around her biceps. 'And this time I'm warning you I'm not letting you go until I'm good and ready.'

The way he said it, all male attitude and arrogance, sent a shiver of excitement along her nerve-endings. Emma heard a whisper of sound issue from her throat an instant before his lips touched hers.

Then she was lost. In his taste: rich and velvety, like the world's finest chocolate. His cool mossy scent mingled with leather. The warmth of his body as he shifted her against him for a closer fit.

She should have stopped it right there, told him no— he'd given her the option. But her response was torn from her like autumn's last leaf in a storm-ravaged forest. Irrational. Irresistible. Irrevocable.

Voices ebbed and flowed in the distance but she barely heard them above the pounding of her pulse, her murmur of approval as she melted against him like butter on a barbecue grill. Her arms slid around his waist to burrow under his jacket, where he was warm and solid through the T-shirt's soft jersey.

Jake felt her resistance soften, her luscious lips grow pliant as she opened for him, giving him full access, and he plunged right in. Dark, decadent delight. Moans and murmurs. Her tongue tangled with his, velvet on satin, and her taste was as sweet as spun sugar.

Dragging her against him, he moved closer, his fingertips tracking down her spine, over the flare of her backside, where he pressed her closer so he could feel her heat.

So she could feel his rapidly growing erection butting against her.

He felt the change instantly—subtle, but sure. A tensing of muscles. A change in her stance. She didn't move away and her lips were still locked with his, but…

Breaking the kiss with a good deal of reluctance, he leaned back to look at her. They were the same age—both twenty-seven—but she looked impossibly young with her hair scraped back from her face, her eyes huge dark pools in the moonlight, her mouth plundered.

He stroked a finger over the groove that had formed between her brows. 'You're thinking too hard.'

'One of us should.' She didn't look away. Nor did the frown smooth out.

'Okay. Talk to me.'

She took a step back. 'This…thing between us is getting way too complicated.'

'Seems pretty straightforward to me. So I'm proposing a deal,' he went on before she could argue, resting his hands on her shoulders. 'This weekend neither of us talks about work.' He touched his forehead to hers. 'We don't *think* about work. We're both between partners, so we'll enjoy the wedding and each other's company…and whatever happens *happens*. No complications. One weekend, Emma.'

'One weekend.' She leaned away, her eyes clouded with conflicting emotions. 'And then what?'

'Put next week out of your mind, it's too far away.'

Come Monday they'd go their separate ways. Back to real life and working ridiculous hours. Emma and the Blue Mountains would be nothing but a warm and pretty memory.

'Think about this instead,' he said, sliding his hands down her upper arms. 'Neither of us wants to be tied down, and we both work our backsides off. We deserve some playtime.'

'Playtime?' She stared up at him, her eyes the colour of the mist-swirled mountains behind her. 'No deal. Not with you.'

'Why not? Afraid you might enjoy yourself?'

She rolled her lips together, as if to stop whatever she'd been about to say, then said, 'I just don't want to play with you, that's all.' She turned and began walking back the way they'd come.

'Liar.' Grabbing her arm, he walked around her, blocking her path until they stood face to face. 'Tell me you didn't enjoy that kiss just now.'

She studied him a moment. 'I didn't enjoy that kiss just now.'

He laughed. 'You started it. That night at the restaurant. You blew me away with your enthusiasm and got me seriously thinking about you. And me. I haven't stopped thinking about you and me—together—since.'

'I told you, that kiss was an overreaction to a particular circumstance,' she said primly. 'And what are we—kids? *"You started it",'* she muttered with a roll of her eyes, but he thought he saw a hint of humour there too.

She looked so delightful he couldn't resist—he planted a firm smacking kiss on those pouted lips then grinned. 'I'd better get you back. Stella'll be starting to think I've kidnapped you.'

Grabbing her hand, he tugged her alongside him along the path towards the hotel. The weekend had barely begun, plenty of time to convince her to change her mind.

'So. Seen any good movies lately?'

She kept up a brisk pace beside him. 'No.'

'Me neither. Stella mentioned you swim every morning, come rain or shine. Is that true?'

'Yes.'

'So...if I were to change my early-morning jog—'

'One weekend.' She jerked to a sudden halt and looked up at him. 'And whatever happens happens?'

A strand of hair had come loose and blew across her eyes. He smoothed it back, tucked it behind her ear. 'We'll take things as they come. It'll be good, I promise.'

Oh, yes, she knew. Emma stared into those beguiling eyes. 'I bet you say that to all the girls.' She couldn't believe she was having this conversation with Jake Carmody.

She resumed walking, hoping she was headed in the right direction. Everything seemed surreal. The moonlight distorting their combined shadows on the path in front of them. The sharp eucalpyt fragrance of the bushland. The way her body was responding to his proximity even now.

His seductive charm really knew no bounds. No wonder women swooned and fell at his feet. She firmed her jaw. Not *this* woman. Still, she didn't have to swoon, exactly...

He was suggesting what amounted to nothing more than a weekend of sex and sin. Heat shimmied down her spine. A weekend on Pleasure Island. She had no doubt Jake could deliver, and couldn't deny the idea called to her on more than one level. But was she game enough? Why not? It wasn't a lifetime commitment, for heaven's sake.

Since her father's death eleven years ago she'd worked her butt off to make things better for them all. Jake had made it clear to her that it was past time she took something for herself. One weekend to be free and irresponsible. And this weekend, with Stella leaving home and the love rat a disappearing blot on her horizon, was it perhaps a good time to start?

They reached the hotel and she hesitated on the shallow steps out front. Her cheeks felt hot and super sensitive, as if a feather might flay away the skin.

She turned to say goodnight and met his gaze. The heat from that kiss still shimmered in his eyes, and it took all her will-power to keep from flinging herself at him and kissing him again.

Deliberately she stepped back, aware she hadn't given him an answer and just as aware they both already knew what her answer would be. She turned towards the building.

A liveried porter swept the wide glass door open with a welcoming smile and warm air swirled out. 'Good evening, madam.'

'Good evening.' She smiled back, wondering if her cheeks and lips were as pink and chapped as they felt. From the safety of distance, she turned to Jake once more. 'Till tomorrow, then.'

'Get a good night's sleep.'

His smile was pure sin. *You'll need it*—no mistaking that message in those hot dark eyes, and her heart turned a high somersault. It continued its gymnastics all the way up the three flights of stairs.

Stella was bundled in a fluffy white hotel robe on the couch, watching a TV cook-off, when she entered.

'Traitor.' But there was no sting in the word as Emma pulled out the fortune cookie note and dropped it on Stella's lap. 'For you.' Because her legs were still wobbly, she flopped down on the couch beside her.

'"Two hearts, one soul." Ooh, I've gone all gooey inside.' Smiling broadly, Stella tucked her legs up beneath her. 'What does yours say?'

She shook her head, that overly warm sensation prickling her skin. 'Never mind.'

Stella stuck out her hand, palm up. 'Come on—give.'

'Oh, for heaven's sake.' Emma dug into her pocket again, then glued her attention to the TV screen, but she wasn't seeing it. 'It's not romantic, like yours. And that's okay because I'm not a romantic like you.' She pressed a fist to her lips to stem the flow.

'"A caress is better than a career." Of course it's romantic, silly. It's telling you to take time out and enjoy... To... *Em.*'

'Where's my computer, by the way? Jake said...never mind.' Emma could feel Stella's gaze on her and jerked herself off the couch without waiting for an answer. 'I'm going to take a bath.'

'Oh. My. Lord.'

'What?' She was in the process of ripping off her tracksuit jacket but stopped at her sister's tone. 'What's wrong?'

Stella was staring at her. And pointing. 'What have you done with my sister?'

'What are you talking about?' She shrugged her shoulders. Ran a hand around her neck. 'What's he done?'

'Ha!' Stella jabbed her finger in the air again. 'I should be asking what *Jake's* done with my sister.'

'No. It's nothing. Don't you say one word to Jake or I'll—'

'*Not* nothing.' Stella craned forward, studying Emma as if she was counting her eyelashes. 'My big sister with fresh whisker burn around her mouth. And stars in her eyes. She's never had stars in her eyes. *Never.*'

'Don't be ridiculous.' Panicked, Emma swiped at her mouth, then sucked in her lips and backed away. Tugged her T-shirt over her head and threw it on her bed. 'Do you know how cold it is outside? The air... A hot bath...'

'Emma Dilemma.' Stella grinned. 'You've just had it on with best man Jake.'

'*No.* It's such a cliché to get it on with the best man. I kissed him, that's all. No. He kissed me. We kissed each other. He started it. No biggie, okay?'

Stella shook her head. 'My sister never gets flustered when she talks about a guy. *Never.*'

Emma fumbled through her suitcase. 'He's not a guy, he's Jake. And I'm not flustered. It's nothing.'

'It's something.'

She yanked her pyjamas from her overnighter and blew out a breath then turned to Stella who was watching her with her chin on the back of the sofa. 'Okay, it's something. But it's just a weekend something. Or not. I haven't decided yet.'

Stella smiled. 'You know you'll have this room all to yourself tomorrow night…?'

'Not another word.' Emma flung up a hand. 'You breathe so much as a syllable of this conversation to Jake or anyone else and I'll sabotage your wedding night.'

And, swiping up her cosmetics bag, she fled to the bathroom.

CHAPTER SEVEN

THE wedding day dawned bright and clear. And cold. Clad in her complimentary terrycloth robe, Emma took her early-morning coffee onto the balcony to admire the cotton balls of cloud that hid the valley floor. From her vantage point she could see the garden below, where even now staff were setting out chairs, toting flower arrangements, twining white ribbon and fairy lights through the trees.

A few moments later Stella stumbled out, hair wild, eyes sparkling. 'Good morning.' She leaned a shoulder against Emma's. 'It's just perfect. Isn't it perfect? Not a cloud in the sky. By afternoon it'll be warm and still sunny. Hopefully… Can you believe I'm getting married in a few hours' time?'

Emma dropped a kiss on her sister's cheek on her way back inside. 'And there's a lot to get through before that happens.' She checked her watch. 'Breakfast is due up in ten minutes. The hairdresser will be here in half an hour.'

With less than an hour to go, the bride's dressing room on the first floor was pandemonium. Underwear, costumes, flowers. A blur of fragrance and colour. Sunshine streamed through the window. Champagne and orange juice in tall flutes sat untouched on a sideboard, along with a plate of finger food.

Stella was with Beth, the wedding planner, and her two assistants—one aiming a video camera and catching the memories. The excitement, the laughter, the nerves.

In one of the full-length mirrors Emma caught a glimpse of her reflection in a strapless bustier. Crimson, with black ribbon laces at the front, it looked like something Scarlett O'Hara would have approved of. She yanked the ribbon tight between her breasts and tied it in a double knot, staring closer.

Wow. She actually had breasts today. Enhanced by the bustier's support, they spilled over the top like something out of a men's magazine. The garment pulled in her waist and flared over her hips, leaving a strip of bare belly and the tiny triangle of matching panties tantalisingly visible. A pair of sheer black stockings came to mid thigh, held up by long black suspenders.

For an instant she almost saw Jake's reflection standing behind her, his eyes smouldering as he leaned over her to dip a finger between—

The tap on her shoulder had her spinning in a panicked one-eighty. 'What?' Her breath whooshed out and her heart skipped a beat. 'Stella. Sorry. I was—'

'A million miles away.'

Not as far as that. 'I'm here. Right here.' She gave a bright smile, then forgot about her erotic meanderings as she gazed at the bride. 'Oh, my! Gorgeous.'

Stella's figure-hugging floor-length Guinevere gown was bottle-green crushed velvet. A dull gold panel insert in the bodice gleamed with tiny emerald beads, replicated on the wide belt cinching in her waist. Full-length sleeves flared wide at the wrist and fell in long soft folds. Her coronet of fresh freesias, tiny roses and featherlike greenery complemented her rich auburn hair.

'You look stunning, Stell. Radiant and stunning. I can't wait to see Lancelot's face when he gets a load of you.'

'Neither can I.' She looked down at Emma, waved a hand. 'Um…are you planning on wearing something over that? I'm sure the guys won't mind, but this is my day and I know it's selfish but I want all the attention.'

'Getting there…' With the help of Annie, one of the assistants, Emma stepped into a voluminous skirt and shimmied into the bodice. 'I told you, Stella. You should have been Scarlett, not me.'

'And I told you already, Scarlett's the brunette. She's playful and coquettish and I really, really wanted you to be that woman today. Whereas Guinevere was pale and intense and totally and unconditionally in love with Lancelot.'

'Well, you'll have that attention,' Emma said, admiring her sister. 'Ryan, not to mention the rest of the male population, won't be able to take his eyes off you.'

Annie slipped buttons into the tiny loops at the back of Emma's dress, then handed her black lace gloves and a parasol.

'Don't forget the bridal bouquet.' Emma passed Stella a simple posy of flowers to match those in her hair. She paused with her sister at the top of the wide sweeping staircase. 'We're a clash of eras, aren't we?'

'We are. But it's going to be fun. For both of us.' Stella squeezed Emma's hand. 'Thank you for helping to make it a perfect day.'

'It's not over, it's just beginning.'

The harp's crystal clear rendition of 'Greensleeves' floated on the air as they arrived at the garden's designated bride spot. At a signal from Beth, the music segued beautifully into Bach's 'Jesu, Joy of Man's Desiring.'

'You're up,' Beth murmured to Emma. 'And don't forget to *smile*.'

She'd taken but a few steps along the petal-strewn manicured lawn when she saw Jake and Ryan up ahead. She forgot about smiling. The garden might look like a fairytale. The costumed guests might look magnificent or they might be naked for all Emma knew, because her peripheral vision had disappeared.

Rhett Butler had never looked so devastating. Black suit, dove-grey waistcoat and dark mottled cravat beneath a snowy starched shirt. His eyes met hers and he smiled. A slow, sexy, come-away-with-me smile.

'*Hi,*' he mouthed.

'*Hi,*' she mouthed back, and, *Oh, help.* Her knees went weak but she seemed to be moving forward. What was wrong with her? No man had ever captivated her this way.

Deliberately freeing her gaze, she aimed her smile at Ryan instead, looking regal in a black tunic and cowled top over silver-grey leggings and black knee-high boots. The Clifton family crest was emblazoned on his tunic— she could make out a lion and a medieval helmet in the black-and-gold embroidery.

Not that he was looking at her; his eyes were for his bride, a few steps behind. As they should be. Emma wondered for a quickened heartbeat how it would feel to have someone look at her that way, with shiny unconditional love. She rejected the thought even as it formed and concentrated on keeping her smile in place, her steps smooth and measured.

Jake's eyes feasted on Emma. The deep colour complemented her lightly tanned complexion. A wide-brimmed hat shaded her face, and he couldn't quite read her eyes, so he contented himself with admiring the seductive cleavage and the way the crimson fabric hugged every delectable curve as she moved closer.

His fingers flexed in anticipation of becoming more intimately acquainted with those curves. How long would it take him to get her out of that dress? To lay her down on the grass right here in the sunshine and plunge into her while the birds sang and the cool wind blew up from the valley....

Then she moved out of his line of sight to take her place beside the bride. Probably just as well, because any longer and it might become obvious to all where his thoughts were.

He turned his attention to Ry and Stella, and watched the couple blindly promise to handcuff themselves to each other till death did them part. A life sentence, no parole. His collar itched on Ry's behalf, and he shifted his shoulders against the tight sensation inside his shirt.

They looked happy enough. But it never lasted. There were exceptions, of course. Ry's parents—Henry VIII with a fake red beard and Anne Boleyn—were holding hands, eyes moist.

He glanced at the girls' mother in her white Grecian goddess robe, looking, as always, eternally constipated. Her marriage disaster had turned her into a bitter and twisted woman. Nevertheless, she was still beautiful. He imagined Emma would look as beautiful in thirty years' time.

But he didn't want to contemplate Emma's lovely face marred with that same perpetually pinched expression, those sparkling sapphire eyes clouded with sadness.

Who in their right mind would take the marriage risk? Only those temporarily blinded by that eternal mystery they called love. Not him, thank God.

Formal photographs followed in the gardens, then on

to the decking overlooking the mountains as the sun lowered, turning the sky golden and the valley purple.

Emma couldn't fault Jake's behaviour. He was the perfect gentleman. The perfect Rhett. He only touched her when the photographer required him to do so. During the five-course meal he was seated next to Ryan at the top table, so conversation between them was limited, but there was a heated glance or two when the bridal couple's heads didn't block the view.

After the speeches guests chatted over music provided by a three-piece orchestra as the desserts began coming out of the kitchen. Anne Boleyn, aka the mother of the groom, made her way to the top table.

'Beautiful ceremony, my darlings. It must be your turn next, Emma.'

'Oh, I don't think so.' Emma smiled back, then lifted her champagne glass and swallowed more than she should considering her duties. 'It's not for me.'

'Ah, you just have to find the right man.'

Smile still in place, Emma set her empty glass on the table with a thunk. 'And isn't that the killer?'

'And Jake?' Ryan's mother smiled in his direction. 'When's some clever woman going to snap you up and make an honest man out of you?'

'Alas for me, fair lady.' He put his hand on his heart. 'You're already taken.'

Laughter from the bridal couple. 'You never know, Em,' Stella murmured into her ear as her new mother-in-law walked back to her chair. 'He could be closer than you think.'

'What I'm thinking is it's about time you two cut that white skyscraper.'

The guests applauded as Stella and Ryan laughed into each other's eyes and fed each other cake. Weddings,

Emma thought. They always whipped up those romantic, dreamy, nostalgic emotions. It was hard not to be caught up in the euphoria.

She deliberately veered from those too-pretty thoughts and watched Karina knock back one glass of champagne after another. Emma pursed her lips, remembering the *Pat Me* sticker she'd discovered stuck to her backside after the hens' night. She narrowed her gaze as Karina plastered herself all over one of Ryan's cousins up against a wall. Weddings also came with too much booze and indiscriminate physical contact.

But when Ryan and Stella took to the floor for the bridal waltz to the seductive beat of 'Dance Me to the End of Love', she knew her own moment of up close was imminent and her legs started to tremble.

Jake rose and held out his hand, his eyes as beguiling as the song. 'I think it's our turn.' Emma caught the undertone in his voice and her whole body thrummed with its underlying message that went way beyond the dance floor and upstairs to that big soft bed.

When he grasped her fingers to lead her into the dance space there was something…different about the contact. And in the centre of the room, when he slid his hand to her back, firm and warm and possessive, she felt as if the floor tilted beneath her feet.

They'd never danced together, and his proximity released a stream of endorphins, stimulating her senses. The throb of the music echoed through her body. His cool green aftershave filled her nostrils. The sensuous brush of his thighs against hers beneath the heavy swish of her full skirt had her breath catching in her throat.

'Sorry,' she muttered, missing a step and trying to create some space between them—she needed it to breathe, and to say, 'I'm not a very good dancer.'

'Lucky for you I am.'

She flicked him a look. 'Lucky for you I'm feeling congenial enough to let you get away with that.'

Was there *anything* in the seductive sciences he wasn't accomplished at? She sincerely doubted it as his palm rubbed a lazy circle over her back, creating a deliciously warm friction and at the same time drawing her closer and causing her to misstep—again.

'Is it the dance, or is something else distracting you, Em?'

How typically arrogant male. But she smiled into his laughing eyes. 'Do men always have sex on their minds?'

His answering grin was unrepentant. 'Pretty much.' He dipped close and lowered his voice. 'It's on your mind too.'

She dragged in a breath that smelled of fine fresh cotton and hot man and tried not to notice. 'I'm finding it hard to concentrate on the steps, that's all.'

As Ryan swept his bride past them Emma saw Stella's eyes twinkling at her and looked away quickly. Apart from the bride and groom and Ryan's parents they were the only couple on the floor. 'People are watching us.'

'And why wouldn't they? You look amazing.' The hand holding hers tightened, and his thumb whisked over hers as he leaned in so that his cheek touched her hair. So that his chest shifted against her breasts. 'You feel amazing,' he murmured into her ear. 'Forget the audience. Listen to the music.'

Forget the music. Listen to the Voice. Her head drifted towards his shoulder, the better to hear it. When other couples joined them on the dance floor he swept her towards the window with its panoramic views. Not that she was interested in any view right now except the one in front of her.

He crooned the song's lyrics about wanting to see her beauty when everyone had gone close against her ear. She nearly melted on the spot. 'You think I've changed my mind?'

'Honey, I don't even need to ask.' His hand tightened around hers and then she realised that couples were swirling around them and they were standing still. And close. That the fingers of her free hand had somehow ended up clinging to the back of his neck. That the song had changed to something more upbeat.

How long had they been standing there? How long had she been showing him exactly how she felt? That those options she'd thought she had were down to one? Somehow she managed to yank herself into the present and remember her bridesmaid duties.

She let her hand slide down the smooth fabric of his jacket, slipped the other one from his grasp. 'I need to go.'

'Are you sure?' He lifted the heavy mass of hair from her shoulder with the back of his fingers and stroked the side of her neck, then linked his arms loosely around her waist, trapping her against him. 'Because I'm kind of enjoying where we are right now.'

She felt a series of little taps track up her spine.

'How many buttons would you say this dress has?' He slipped the top one from its tiny loop. Then another.

Her breath caught and her blood fizzed through her veins like hot champagne. 'What do you think you're doing?'

He swirled a finger beneath the fabric. 'Your skin feels like warm satin. How many buttons?' he asked again.

'Twenty two.'

He muttered a soft short word under his breath.

'Is that a problem?'

His eyes burned into hers. 'I've never encountered a

problem with female clothing I couldn't solve one way or another.' And with a slow sexy grin he released her. 'Okay, you're free. For now.'

For now? But she couldn't deny the thrill of knowing he wanted her. That he was already figuring a way to get her out of her dress. That the women casting admiring glances his way were not even on his radar tonight—Emma Byrne was.

His proprietorial hand at her back manoeuvred her through the dancers as she made her way towards the bridal table. A middle aged Fred and Wilma Flintstone twirled by, a gay couple dressed as King Arthur and Merlin, a Beauty and a Beast.

'Who's the Roman warrior chatting up Bernice?'

Emma followed Jake's gaze to a nearby table and snorted a half laugh. 'He won't get far with Mum.' But to her surprise her mother smiled at something the middle-aged guy said. Then laughed. 'Amazing.' Emma smiled too. 'Maybe I should invite him around some time as a distraction when I'm fed up with her.'

'Hang on—that's Ryan's Uncle Stan from Melbourne. Divorced last year and looking good. Go, Stan.'

Emma took that moment to break away. 'I have something I need to take care of.'

Leaving the sounds of laughter and music behind, she made her way to the honeymoon suite in another wing of the hotel with a basket of rose petals. A glance at her watch told her she had half an hour before the happy couple were due to leave the party and celebrate the end of their special day.

More than enough time to catch her breath and take a moment. Letting herself in with the keycard she'd been given at Reception, Emma flicked on the light. A soft glow filled the room, glinting on the massive brass bed and lending a rich luxury to the sumptuous gold and burgundy furnishings. She leaned a shoulder against the door, drawing in air. She really needed to increase her daily workout.

Rubbish. Emma knew her lack of fitness wasn't the reason her lungs felt as if they'd shrunk two sizes. She could try telling herself her underwear was laced too tightly. The ballroom had been badly ventilated. She'd had too much of the fizzy stuff.

But there was only one reason, and thank God he was downstairs—

'Need a hand?'

That familiar seductive drawl coated the back of her neck like hot honey, causing her to jolt and drop her little basket. She drew in a ragged breath. His question, which wasn't a question at all, could only mean one thing, and it wasn't an offer to help sprinkle her rose petals over the quilt.

'Jake...' The word turned into a moan as a warm mouth bit lightly into the sensitive spot where shoulder met neck. She simply didn't have the strength or the will to pull away. 'What are you doing here?'

He soothed the tender spot with his tongue and her toes curled up. 'What do you think I'm doing here?' In one fluid move he spun her around. The door swung shut behind them and he rolled her against the wall, his hands hard and hot and heavy on her shoulders.

He didn't give her time to answer or to think. One instant she was staring into a pair of heavy-lidded dark eyes, the next her mouth was being plundered by the wickedest pair of lips this side of the Yellow Brick Road.

He lifted his mouth a fraction and his breath whispered against her lips. 'Is that clear enough?'

Perfectly. And just clear enough to have her remember where they were and what she'd come here to do. 'Are you out of your mind?' She pushed at his chest. Uselessly. 'Housekeeping could show up here any minute.'

'Then we've got a minute.' He grinned, dark eyes glinting. 'Better make the most of it.'

Excitement whipped through her as his hands rushed down, his thumbs whisking over taut nipples, the heat of his palms searing her skin through the satin as he moulded them around her waist and over her belly with murmurs of appreciation.

There was nothing of the suave, sophisticated gentleman from this afternoon except perhaps the scent of his aftershave. This man was the wickedly handsome rogue bent on seduction that she'd always known him to be. Nothing for her to do but to look into those eyes and oh-so-willingly acquiesce.

He gathered handfuls of her voluminous skirt in his fists at either side of her, creating a cool draught around her knees as he ruched the fabric higher. 'Do you want to tell me to stop?' he murmured, leaning down to sip at her collarbone.

Only to stop wasting time. A moan escaped as the tips of his fingers grazed the tops of her stockings, then came into smooth contact with naked flesh. He slid one sensuous finger beneath a suspender and up, to track along the edge of her panties.

He grinned again as he tossed her skirt up over her breasts. 'How many layers have you got on under here?'

'I don't remember...' Moisture pooled between her legs, dampening her silk knickers, and she didn't know how much longer she could remain upright.

He watched her eyes while his finger cruised closer, curling inward, between her thighs, along the lacy edge of her knickers, almost but never quite touching where she wanted him to touch her most. And the spark she saw in his gaze ignited a burn that wasn't about to be extinguished any time soon.

'Jake…Housekeeping—'

'Tell me what you like. What you want.'

The husky demand turned her mind to mush, and she arched wantonly against his hand. Forget Housekeeping. 'Anything. Everything.' Clutching her skirt, she let her spinning head fall back against the door. 'And quickly.'

He stepped between her legs, the sides of his shoes pushing her feet wider. One sharp tug. Two. The sound of fabric ripping. And she felt her knickers being whisked away from her body by impatient hands.

She trembled. She sighed. She hissed out a breath between her teeth. 'Hurry.'

'No.' His thumb found her throbbing centre. 'A job worth doing…'

'Ah, *yesss…*' A slow, sensuous glide over her swollen flesh—one touch—and the burn became a raging inferno. *So* worth doing…

How could one finger cause such utter devastation? Her eyes slid closed. Golden orbs pulsed across her vision. She felt as if she was standing on the rim of a volcano, yet she was the one about to erupt.

He touched her a second time, and she flew over the edge and into the hot and airless vortex, her inner muscles clamping around him.

She flattened her palms against the wall for balance, her breathing fast and harsh. She felt him step away on a draught of air, and opened her eyes in time to see him grin with promises yet to be fulfilled as he slipped out through the door.

CHAPTER EIGHT

Oh...My. God. Emma sucked in a much needed calming breath. If she'd had the luxury of time she'd have slid down the wall and possibly passed out for the rest of the night.

He'd touched her twice. *Twice.* That was all it had taken to bring her to the most intense orgasm of her life. And then he'd nicked off like some pirate in the night, stealing her breath and her composure and leaving her with the possibility of facing Housekeeping alone.

Out. She realised she was still clutching her skirt up to her chest and pushed it down quickly, her cheeks flaming, at the same time thanking her lucky stars that no one had turned up yet.

A hank of hair fell over one side of her face. She pushed it behind her ear. Panicked all over again, she scanned the floor for her knickers. No sign of them. Picking up her forgotten basket, she stumbled to the bed and dumped the petals in the centre, arranging them in a hasty circle. She placed the two heart-shaped soaps she'd made with Ryan's and Stella's names in gold leaf in the centre, then made her way quickly downstairs, where the couple were preparing to farewell the guests.

She didn't see Jake amongst the crowd until he appeared in the doorway ten minutes later. Their gazes clashed hotly across the room. He was the only one who knew she was naked beneath her gown and her cheeks flamed anew. She prayed he'd stay away from her for the next little while, because they both had their respective duties before the social part of the evening was over.

Neatly sidestepping as Stella threw her bouquet in Emma's direction—she wasn't falling for that old trick—she saw Jake follow the bridal couple out.

She moved among the guests, catching up with friends and relatives. She was on tenterhooks, expecting Jake to tap her on the shoulder at any moment, and she didn't know how she was going to hide the guilty pleasure from her expression.

The band was still playing and guests lingered, enjoying the music. Some danced; others gravitated towards the bar next to the lobby. A while later, when Jake still hadn't shown his face, the glow cooled, to be replaced by an anxious fluttering in the pit of her stomach. Was he coming back? Was he expecting *her* to look for *him* after his impromptu seduction?

She didn't know what game they were playing—had no idea of the rules. *Damn him.* Collecting her hat and parasol from behind the concierge's desk, she made her way towards the bar.

Jake waved Ry and Stella off and headed straight for Reception. Business taken care of there, he stopped to collect a couple of sightseeing brochures on his way to the lobby bar.

He found a comfortable armchair in the corner, from where he could see the ballroom, and signalled the waiter. He knew Emma was still in there. He'd give her some space but if she didn't materialise in ten minutes he was damn well going in there and hauling her out.

Folding the brochures, he slid them into his jacket

pocket. His fingers collided with silk. Emma's panties. He remembered her surprise, the passion in those deep blue eyes, when he'd stripped them off. The way her lips had parted on a moan of pleasure when he'd first touched that intimate flesh.

His body tightened all over again. The next time Emma writhed and moaned against him... He smiled to himself in anticipation. He had definite plans for the way their evening was going to go.

Han Solo and Princess Leia exited, with a lone cowboy in tow. No sign of Emma. He exhaled sharply through his nostrils and rechecked his watch. Was she saying a personal goodnight to everyone in the bloody ballroom?

His order arrived with a paper napkin and a bowl of peanuts. He set the unopened bottle of champagne and two glasses on the floor beside his chair and reached for his beer.

'Good evening, Rhett.'

Jake took a second or two to catch on that the sultry come-hither voice was directed at him. He glanced up to see a well-endowed woman in her mid-thirties or thereabouts, in an embroidered medieval get-up, holding a cocktail glass brimming with blue liquid and a cherry on a stick.

He lifted his glass and drained half of it down then set it back on the table. 'Hi.'

She took his half-smile as an invitation and spread herself out on the chair opposite him, placing her glass up close to his. She lifted the little stick to her mouth.

'So.' He kept his eyes off the cleavage obviously on offer and leaned back, crossed his legs. 'Who are you tonight?'

Slipping the cherry between her glossed lips, she tossed her mane of auburn hair over her shoulder and aimed a killer smile at him. 'The Lady of Shalott.'

He took his time to say, 'No Mr Shalott?'

She giggled. The sound grated the way feet scrabbling down a rubbled cliff face to certain death grated. Clearly she thought he was interested in her as the night's entertainment. And at some other time he might have been interested. Or not.

'There *was* no Mr Shalott. It's a poem,' she informed him, in case he didn't know.

'Yes, Tennyson. Tragic circumstances. The girl loved Lancelot but he really wasn't that into her, was he?'

She leaned forward on the edge of her chair. 'But he didn't *know* her. If he'd taken the time, things might've turned out different.'

'But not necessarily for the better. Lancelot had his eye on someone else. The lady would've been disappointed.' A thought occurred to him and he tried to recall if he knew her. 'You and Ry weren't…?' He jiggled a hand in front of them.

She grinned. 'No. I had no idea the groom was going to be Lancelot. I'm Ryan's cousin. Kylie. From Adelaide.'

'Ah…yes. Cousin Kylie from Adelaide.'

He'd heard about Wily Kylie—two husbands down, on the prowl for her third. He suddenly needed a drink, and lifted his beer.

Following suit, Kylie raised her glass and tapped it to his. Her eyes drifted to his mouth. 'To a good night.'

Not if I hang around here it won't be. Like an addict, he suddenly craved the woman he'd partnered all day, not this silicone bimbo looking for rich husband number three. *Emma.* A woman with a real body and a smile that could quite possibly melt his heart if he wasn't careful.

'And a good night to you too.' He drained the glass and set it down on the napkin, then picked up his bottle and glasses, rose and executed a bow. 'Welcome to Sydney, Lady Kylie, enjoy your stay.'

He didn't wait for a reply, simply turned on his heel and headed towards the ballroom to find Emma.

Emma's hands shook so much she could barely swipe the keycard through its slot. On the third try she managed to let herself in and lean back against the door. She felt physically ill—as if the five-tiered wedding cake had lodged in her stomach.

One hand clenched on her parasol, she rubbed her free hand over her heart and up her throat. Jake hadn't come near her since their upstairs 'encounter'. For want of a better word. Never mind that she'd stupidly tried to avoid him; that was totally beside the point.

Flinging her hat into the air, she watched it sail across the room. She'd been hanging around in the ballroom, expecting him to come and find her. But he hadn't. When it came to guys like him she really was *so* naïve.

Then *she'd* found *him.* In the lobby bar…with a woman who *looked* like a woman, not some under-developed teenager.

The soft knock at the door behind her had her whirling around. Heart pounding in her throat, she yanked the door open.

Jake leaned on the doorjamb, his jacket slung over one shoulder, shirtsleeves rolled back. His hair was a little mussed, his cravat was gone, and the top button of his shirt was undone, leaving his throat tantalisingly exposed. He dangled a bottle of champagne and two glasses in his free hand.

His eyes met hers. They burned with such hot, unsatisfied hunger her throat closed over and she couldn't raise so much as a whisper. All she could think was he'd come for her. *Her.*

He lifted the bottle. 'You going to let me in? Or do you want the entire floor to know the best man's planning a hot night with the bridesmaid?' He grinned as he slid sideways and passed her, brushing his liquor-tinged lips over hers on his way. 'I hope you hadn't planned on starting without me.'

She took a moment to catch his meaning, then a wild fire swept up her neck and into her cheeks. All she managed was a gurgling sound at the back of her throat.

She closed the door and leaned back against it, heart pounding as she watched him toss his jacket over the couch, watched the way his muscles bunched beneath his shirt. His hair held the gleam of burnished gold threads amongst the brown.

He glanced back at her as he walked to a little round table topped with a crystal vase of fresh blooms. 'You weren't running out on me, were you?'

'You...you were otherwise occupied.' She found her voice.

He frowned. 'I was *waiting* for you.'

'I didn't know.' The door felt hard, the row of buttons digging into her spine.

He set the bottle and glasses down, brows raised, eyes dark as midnight. 'You *didn't know?* Jeez, woman.'

'I thought maybe you'd...' *found someone more desirable, more attractive* '...changed your mind.'

'What? This weekend's about you and me, remember?'

Her chin lifted. 'I never agreed.' Exactly.

'You...' He shook his head, eyes changing, finally comprehending. 'Come on, Emma, do you really think I'd go for that type downstairs?'

'I...hoped not.' She swallowed, relief softening her

limbs, and allowed herself a smile. 'Because then I'd have to hit you with my parasol.'

He grinned back at her, eyes wicked. 'Maybe I'll let you. Later.'

'Um…' Was she really up for an experienced man like Jake?

He popped the cork off the champagne bottle. 'Tonight's been a foregone conclusion all along, and we both know it.'

Yes. And for this moment, for what was left of the weekend, or for however long this spark burned, she knew without a doubt she wanted to make love with Jake more than her next breath.

He set the bottle down. 'Come here and kiss me.'

She needed no second bidding. Crossing the few steps between them, she flattened herself against his chest, her arms circling his neck, fingers diving into his hair as she fused her mouth to his.

Heat met heat. Not sweet and tender—not even close. Not with Jake. Nor did she want it so. This melding of selves and mashing of lips was a dark, dangerous mix of pent-up passion and long-held desires. Exactly what she wanted.

Hard hands dragged her closer, then zigged down her spine to press her bottom against him so that she could feel the steel ridge of his erection. Persuasive pressure. Promised delights.

He lifted his lips to murmur, 'Emma, Emma, you've been driving me crazy all evening. All week.'

His admission thrilled her to her toes. 'Same goes…' Dazed and dizzy, she arched her hips against his hardness and clung to him, welcoming the scrape of evening beard as he worked his lips and teeth up her throat, down the side of her neck, over her décolletage.

Impatient hands skimmed over her breasts, kneading and squeezing, deft fingers finding her aching nipples through the satin and rolling them into hardened peaks.

The delicate fragrance of the valley's sweet-scented wattle and eucalypt from the arrangement on the table mingled with the hot scent of aroused man as he laved the swell of her breasts above the neckline of her dress, then bent his head lower to nip and suck at her nipples through the fabric.

He made a sound of frustration, lifted his head and leaned back slightly to look at her. Light from the chandelier wall bracket glinted in his eyes, but the heat, the purpose she saw there, burned with its own fire.

'How many buttons did you say?'

Oh. 'Buttons…' She raised her arms to help but he didn't give her time. In a frenzy of movement, he fisted his hands in the fabric at her shoulders and yanked. She felt the satin give way down her back as buttons popped and pinged. 'Uh…'

'I know a dressmaker…'

Of course he did.

Dropping to his knees, he pushed the ruined garment and accompanying petticoats to her feet. She stepped out of the mound of puddled satin, kicked it away, leaving her wearing nothing but her laced bustier and stockings.

'You're gorgeous,' he murmured, voice husky. A corner of his mouth kicked up in a wry smile. 'And armour-plated yet again.'

Goosebumps of heat followed his gaze as it swept up her corset-trapped body to meet her eyes. 'Not quite. You do have my panties…don't you?' she finished on a slightly panicked note.

'They're mine now.' He looked down at the feminine

secrets exposed below the suspenders, then back, his eyes burning. 'I want to see all of you.'

He knelt in front of her, took off her shoes then un-hitched her stockings, warm hands gliding them down her legs, breath hot on her naked skin. She lifted each foot so he could slide them off and toss them away.

Hands shaking, she started to fumble for the laces. Her breasts weren't... 'I'm not—'

Laying a finger on her lips, he shook his head.

Taking her hands in his, he spread them wide so that their bodies bumped in all the right places, then, fingers entwined, brought them in close and began to waltz. Tiny steps, his thighs pressing against hers. He swayed her towards the massive four-poster bed. She could almost hear the dusky beat of Stella's chosen song that they'd danced to earlier.

She felt the corner of the bed against her thighs as he backed her up against the bedpost. Watching her, he turned her hands palm up, kissed the inside of each wrist, where her pulse beat a rock concert's applause, then curled each finger around the smooth wooden bedpost above her head.

'And don't let go,' he ordered, squeezing them for good measure, fingers trailing down her raised arms, leaving little shivers sparkling in their wake.

The erotic pose triggered within her an avalanche of wild needs and urgent demands. Her breasts thrust upwards, straining at the bustier's confines, nipples tight to the point of pain and on fire for his touch.

'Jake...' She sighed. Wanting it all. Wanting it now.

His eyes swept over her and his smooth seduction vanished in the blink of an eye.

His fingers scrambled for the laces. When she loosened her hold on the post in a frantic effort to hasten the process he grabbed her wrists, pinning her in place, a firestorm in his dark gaze. *'Stay.'*

A thrill spiralled through her body, clenching low in her belly as he renewed his task. His hands weren't steady, she noticed, and his breathing was ragged. He swore, then a hand dived into his trouser pocket and reappeared with a miniature Swiss Army knife. A handful of condoms spilled onto the floor.

She glanced down at them, then met his eyes. 'Boy Scout?'

'Just prepared,' he muttered thickly.

His eyes darkened. She knew his intent, and her pulse kicked into a wild erratic rhythm. No trace of the suave urban sophisticate—just prime, primitive male. She loved that he'd lost control with *her*—plain and ordinary Emma Byrne.

He flicked the tiny blade open and nicked the first ribbon. The second. Her breath sucked in. So did her stomach. His knuckles grazed a nipple as he worked his way down. The erotic response echoed in her womb, drawing it tight at the same time softening and moistening the internal muscles, slackening her inner thighs.

'Jake…'

Snick, snick, snick. 'I'll buy you another one.'

'Doesn't…matter…it's…only ribbon.'

The undergarment fell apart and slid to the floor and her breasts spilled free. And suddenly it didn't matter that she didn't have the breasts she'd like to have, because he was looking at them with awe and appreciation.

'Gorgeous,' he whispered. 'Absolutely perfect.'

Dropping the knife, he filled his hands with her, thumbs whisking over the tight buds, rolling and pinching them between his fingers until she thought she'd pass out with the pleasure. Wayne had never, *never* worshipped her body the way Jake was doing.

She writhed against the post, tilting her hips and arching her back. Closer…she had to get closer… She needed more. Him inside her. *Now.*

A groan rumbled up his throat and she heard the sharp rasp of his zipper. Without taking his eyes off hers, he somehow produced a condom that hadn't fallen from his pocket and ripped the foil packet open with his teeth.

Her breath stalled in her throat as he quickly sheathed himself. 'Hurry.' Anticipation and that aching, devastating need had reached flashpoint.

Hard wide palms clamped onto her hips, a sensuous vice, holding her in place. With unerring precision he plunged deep and hard and true. A torpedo finding its target. Invading her, stretching her, filling her.

Where he belonged.

Somewhere in a dark corner of her pleasure-fogged mind she fought that concept even as she embraced it. Then all thought melted into oblivion as she gave herself wholly over to layer after layer of sensation.

His hard thighs abraded hers through the rough weave of his trousers while he hammered into her. The sound of his laboured breaths, shockingly harsh in the room's stillness, and her own rapid sighs of response.

The golden light pulsing behind her eyes as she felt her climax building, building… Her legs threatening to give way, she clung tighter to the satin-smooth pole behind her, then Jake's hands were covering hers, holding her upright. From heads to toes their bodies collided, naked skin to fully clothed.

She was slick, hot and unbearably erotic, and Jake couldn't remember the last time he'd been so turned on. She bucked against him, all wild, wanton woman, meeting his thrusts with an eagerness and energy that rivalled his own.

He hadn't expected Emma to be so utterly responsive, and the pleasure of it, of *her,* slapped through him, sharp and viciously arousing. Clenching her hands between his own he drove into her, the urge to plunder and possess riding roughshod over anything sane and rational.

He'd not known it could be like this. That need for a woman—for one woman—could be so desperate, so powerful, so consuming. Some kind of madness had seized him.

She came in a rush, all but sobbing his name, her internal muscles clamping around him, silky walls of heat that triggered his own climax.

Their joined hands slid down the sweat-slicked post and he released her, and they flopped onto the bottom of the bed together in a tangle of sated limbs, their ragged breaths filling the air.

'Come here,' he murmured when he felt able enough to move again, shifting up the bed and dragging her with him. He hauled her on top and she lay spread-eagled over his body like one of those ragdoll cats. Against his thundering heart, he felt hers pounding in unison.

'Do you realise this is the first time we've actually been horizontal together?' she said drowsily.

'Mmm,' he answered, almost as lazily. Her body fitted seamlessly against his, curves to angles, womanly soft where he was hard, as if she'd been made exclusively for him. She made him feel like the king of the universe. Already he was becoming aroused again, his body stirring as she arched a bare foot over his calf.

'Hey, you gonna get naked with me or what?' Her voice was slurred with fatigue.

He tilted her face so he could look at her, skin peach-perfect and sheened with a translucent film of moisture, eyes still glazed with residual passion.

Emma.

An unfamiliar feeling stole through him. One he wasn't sure how to deal with. He eased her off to one side. Her hair was in disarray; he smoothed it away from her face and kissed her damp brow. 'Give me a minute.'

In the bathroom he dealt with the condom, then splashed cold water on his face. He'd just had wild sex with Emma. *Emma.* Looking away from the frown he glimpsed in his reflection, he swiped a towel and dried his face.

When he came back she'd burrowed beneath the quilt and was fast asleep, dead centre in the middle of the bed, one arm flung across a pillow, long dark lashes resting on cheeks the colour of dawn.

She looked tiny, all alone in that master bed. As if the snowy mountain of quilt might swallow her up.

Vulnerable.

That odd feeling intensified. He watched the slow rise and fall of the quilt as she breathed. He'd not anticipated this...this surge of emotion. What had he done?

He should go back to his own room, he thought, even as he stripped off his shirt, tossed it over the chair. Collect a few essentials. She might need some space. Hell, *he* needed some space.

But he toed his shoes off, shoved down his trousers and jocks and stepped out of them. Retrieved the condoms from the floor, dropped them on the nightstand, then slipped into bed beside her.

She snuggled against him with a sleep murmur. Her warmth seeped into his bones, her exotic fragrance...fresh and floral and exclusively hers, surrounded him. He'd never forget that exotic fragrance. And when this attraction had run its course...

He closed his eyes.

Tomorrow. He'd think about that tomorrow.

CHAPTER NINE

THE sound of a man's steady breathing woke Emma. A hard-muscled, hairy thigh was draped over one leg, its weight effectively pinning the lower half of her body in place. A warm hand curved around her left breast.

Jake.

Her heart leapt and her body burned as images of last night with the man of her dreams flooded back. She knew it was morning because a dull apricot light shimmered behind her eyelids, but she didn't open her eyes. She lay still, not wanting him to wake yet, because she wanted to replay every glorious, mind-blowing minute. Her skin felt as if it had been rubbed all over with a stiff towel.

He'd made love to her again while the soft darkness co-cooned them in its blanket of intimacy. Horizontally this time. And slowly, skilfully. Sinfully. The way only a man with Jake's experience could.

And again and again. Always different, always amazing.

Her eyes blinked open and she turned her head on the pillow to study him. As innocent as a baby but she knew better. Those perfectly sculpted lips, so relaxed in sleep, could wreak absolute havoc. Everywhere. A quicksilver shiver ran through her.

His hair was sticking up and it was an odd feeling knowing she'd had something to do with it. She smiled to herself. She itched to run her fingers through its silky softness again. Couldn't wait to feel the weight of his body on hers, to feel him come inside her again. Now. Tonight. Next week.

But reality intruded like a thief, stealing away the lovely feeling and her smile faded. This weekend was all he'd offered. All they'd agreed on. Just for fun.

And that was all she wanted too, right?

So make the most of it, she told herself, determined to ignore the feeling tugging at her and pleading for more. *Live in the moment.* They still had a late checkout and the rest of the day to spend together however they chose. A lot of fun could be packed into those few hours.

Easing her leg from beneath his, she slid a hand down between smooth sheets and hard-muscled belly... She found him semi-erect and wrapped her fingers around him. His eyes snapped open and that innocence disappeared in an instant, replaced with hot, not-quite-sleepy desire as he hardened beneath her palm.

'Good morning,' she murmured, and slid her hand down his satin-steel length and up again. 'Sorry to wake you... Actually, I'm not sorry.' She squeezed gently. 'I've got big plans for the day.'

He stuck one hand behind his head and watched her. A smile teased the corners of his mouth. 'Have you, now?'

'Mmm.' Positioning her top half over his chest, she rubbed against him once, twice, enjoying the rasp of masculine hair against her nipples, before reaching down to cup the heavy masculinity between his thighs. *Very big plans.* Resting her chin on his breastbone, she looked into his eyes. 'What about you? Any ideas?'

'I'm up for anything.' His smile was wicked and wide awake, like the rest of him.

She pushed the quilt down and took her time to admire the magnificent view of tanned skin over hard-packed muscle...and the proud, arrogant jut of his masculinity. 'I noticed.' Before he could flip her on her back and have her at his mercy again, she took charge and straddled him, reaching for a condom. 'Let's start the day on a high.'

A short while later, snuggled against him, she stretched lazily. Sunday mornings didn't get any better than this.

'Speaking of high,' Jake said, running his fingertips up and down her arm. 'What else are you up for today, Emma?'

A sneaky premonition snaked down her spine. 'Depends.'

'I'm thinking there's a playground of world-famous tourist attractions within walking distance that we should make the most of.'

She knew, and her stomach was already doing somersaults. Did she want to be suspended two hundred and seventy metres above the forest floor on a wire cable? Or be slung down the side of a cliff on the steepest funicular railway in the world?

Her whole body recoiled. She wasn't a fan of heights and she didn't care who knew it. 'Or we could explore the local galleries, or take a drive to Leura and have lunch in one of the cafés before we head home,' she suggested hopefully.

He grinned and shook his head. 'Come on, Em, where's your sense of adventure?'

'I lost it somewhere. Really,' she insisted, when his grin remained. If anything it broadened. 'I think maybe I used it all up in this room,' she finished. She stared at him, her whole body blushing at everything they'd gotten up to last night. Suddenly feeling way too naked, she sat up, pulling the sheet over her breasts. 'Is this...*us*...weird?'

His grin faded, and for a long moment he didn't answer while they watched each other. In the stretched silence she heard a service trolley lumber past the room, the clatter of dishes. Had she ever seen his eyes so dark? Something behind that gaze had her heart stumbling around inside her chest… It was supposed to be just physical. *A week-end on Pleasure Island, remember?*

'You're thinking too hard again.' Jake reached out, smoothed her hair behind her ear. 'I rebooked my room. I want another night with you. What do you say?'

Yes, please?

One more night. Her pulse was on a fast track up the side of that mountain. Free and irresponsible was calling her, and she wasn't ready to go back to her boring job and busy *unsociable* life just yet.

'It'll mean a very early start tomorrow if we're going to make it to the city in time.'

'I've decided to take tomorrow off. You?'

'Monday's busy. I've got—'

'Stay with me. Call in sick.'

'I can't just take a day off.'

His brows rose. 'Why the hell not? Your sister just got married. Your boss'll understand.' His voice turned low and smooth and seductive. 'If you want, I can convince him you need the day to recover.'

She frowned. How she chose to use her recreational time was one thing, her job was quite another. An income was a necessity. A one-night stand, even a two-night stand, was a luxury.

And didn't every woman deserve a little luxury now and again?

Still… 'I haven't interfered in your working life, Jake. Please respect mine. And, just so you know, my boss is a woman, and it happens she's a real soft touch when it comes to love and romance.' She leant over and soothed his lips with hers. 'I'll organise it myself.' And deal with the repercussions later.

'Good decision.' She felt his fingers on the back of her head, holding her still while he turned her smooch into a meltingly irresistible kiss.

'Are *you?*' he murmured against her lips a moment later.

'Am I what?'

'A soft touch when it comes to love and romance. You feel soft enough...' He drifted a finger over her cheek, a bare shoulder.

She drew back, shrugged off the words and the associated emotions she didn't want or need. Jake and love and romance were mutually exclusive. In that they were equally matched. But she couldn't quite look him in the eye, and drew circles on the crisp pillow-case with a fingertip. 'I don't want the complication of either in my life.'

'You're a career girl.'

'At least you can count on your career.' Unlike counting on a man.

'Okay, career girl. We'll both play hooky tomorrow and then take a leisurely drive back to town.' He sat up, swung his legs over the side of the bed and reached for his trousers on the floor. 'I need to go back to my room, take a shower and change. Meet me downstairs for breakfast in half an hour and we'll discuss our plans.'

'Okay.' She watched him pull last night's clothes over his magnificent taut backside. The way the muscles in his shoulders bunched as he shrugged into his shirt. Biting back a sigh, she rose and picked up the terrycloth robe she'd worn the night before, which still lay on a nearby chair. She tied the sash and followed him to the door.

'See you in a little while,' he said, bending to kiss her

before opening the door. Then Emma saw his shoulders tense as he came to an abrupt halt.

'Jake.'

She heard her mother's chipped ice voice and Emma's skin flushed to the roots of her tousled bedroom hair. Shrinking into her robe, she hugged the lapels up to her chin with both hands.

'Good morning, Bernice.' Jake's back was towards Emma, and if he was surprised or embarrassed his voice gave no sign. 'Em's about to take a shower,' she heard him say as he sauntered out, his jacket and waistcoat slung over a shoulder. 'You just caught her in time.'

Emma sucked in a fortifying breath. 'Mum.' She moved forward and pulled the door wider while she imagined slamming it shut. 'Jake was…just leaving.' Obviously. And he seemed to have taken her thought-processing skills with him.

Her mother stalked in, missing none of last night's carnage strewn across the floor. 'I came to tell you I'm driving back with Ryan's Uncle Stan.'

Was that a flicker of *excitement* in her mother's eyes? But when Emma blinked it had vanished. 'That's…great, Mum…' She trailed off. What to say?

'I wanted to make sure you'd arranged a lift, but I assume now that you're driving back with Jake.'

Emma heard the underlying criticism loud and clear. 'Thanks, but actually I'm staying on another night.' Defiance streamed through her veins. 'Make that *we're* staying another night.'

Her mother had been staring at the rumpled bed but she swung to face her. 'What about work tomorrow morning?'

'I'm taking the day off.'

'Have you no sense of responsibility, girl? And with

a man like Jake.' She exhaled her disapproval audibly through pinched nostrils.

'I never take time off. As for Jake, I like him, Mum. And so does Stella.' She hugged her arms to ward off the chill in her mother's eyes. 'He's an interesting, honest, hard-working man. I make my own decisions about the men I choose to see. And my own mistakes.'

'So you already think he's a mistake, then?'

Maybe it *was* a mistake, but she'd never know if she didn't take the risk. Jake had liberated something inside her last night and she wanted explore it, even if it was only for what was left of the weekend. 'I want a chance to find out.'

'Very well, then,' her mother replied, tight-lipped. The stony expression remained as she moved to the door. 'I'll see you at home.'

'Right. Drive safely.' Emma maintained an outward calm until the door closed with chilling formality, then swung around to lean back against it and slap her palms on the smooth wood. And a big goodbye to allowing her mother to put a blot on the morning.

It was only a little risk, she told herself, gathering her discarded garments and all the loose buttons she could locate. She tossed them into her suitcase, took out her casual clothes. A relaxing day playing tourist in the Blue Mountains was just what she needed.

And tonight... Her newly energised body tightened at the thought. It was going to be fun. Just fun.

CHAPTER TEN

AFTER waving the newly married couple off on their honeymoon, Jake convinced Emma to walk to Echo Point again later that morning. The air was cold but the sun was out for now, turning the Three Sisters a stark orange against the blue-tinged foliage. A bank of clouds was building; it would rain before nightfall.

'So Stan's driving your mum home,' Jake said as they gazed over the valley. Bernice finding him in Emma's room had been an unexpected and awkward moment. 'Did she give you a hard time?' Neither of them had spoken of the episode over breakfast, but it needed to be said.

'No more than usual.' Emma spoke casually, but he saw her posture dip as she leaned on the railing as if it might prop her up. 'I hope Stan can put her in a better mood.'

'If anyone can cheer Bernice up, Stan's your man.'

Hanging on to the rail with both hands, she leaned back at a crazy angle and looked at the sky. 'You know what? I don't want to think about her *or* work today.'

'Good girl.' He covered her hands with his. 'Today's for us.'

'Sounds perfect.' Turning to him, she tipped her face up to his, last night's sparkle still dancing in her eyes. She wore a faded tracksuit, scuffed sneakers and her hair was tied back into a loose coil which hung between her shoulderblades. Without make-up, her face glowed with good health except for some luscious-looking peach-coloured lipgloss.

She looked...radiant. Last night's gymnastics had done her a world of good. 'Let's go.' Keeping her hand clasped firmly in his, he headed towards a walking trail which pointed to Katoomba Falls.

Seeing the spectacular World Heritage sights with Emma, he discovered their mutual enjoyment of exploring nature on foot. She shared his interest in the environment and the native flora and fauna they came across. Ancient ferns, rainbow lorikeets. They even glimpsed an echidna fossicking in the bushland nearby.

He persuaded her to cross the valley on the Skyway with the promise of lunch at the revolving restaurant at the other end. She buried her face against his chest as they swung out into space so high that the shadow of their cabin was the size of a newborn's thumbnail on the Jurassic forest below.

Jake couldn't remember a day he'd enjoyed more in a long time. Simple things like sharing a can of soda while they sat on a rock with the breeze at their backs and listened to the crystal sounds of the nearby Katoomba waterfall.

He was as interested in Emma's mind and her opinions as he was in her body. Connecting with her, seeing that rare smile and finding out what they had in common, was as much a part of the day as the hot, lingering looks they exchanged, knowing the evening ahead promised to be as special as the last.

By mid-afternoon it was becoming increasingly difficult to keep his hands off her, so they cut the sightseeing short and made a fast trip back to the hotel and his suite.

Later, surrounded by white candles in the gleaming

black spa of the stunning black bathroom, with its wide uninterrupted view, they sipped bubbly and watched the constantly changing panorama. A curtain of rain filled the valley floor, a blur of dull gold with the setting sun behind as the shower moved through in brilliant contrast to the encroaching stormy black sky.

But the best view was right in front of him.

Emma's hair was catching the sun's last feeble rays, and the soft glow of candlelight shone on her cheeks as day-light faded.

She was facing him across a mountain of bubbles, and in those sapphire eyes, with their stars and luminosity, he could see a load had been lifted. She'd let herself go for once in her life and had a good time.

How long would it take for the pressures of real life to tarnish that glow and eclipse the sparkle? After tomorrow's short return journey to the urban rat race it was back to business for them both.

Which made it all the more important not to waste a single second of what was left of tonight.

He took her glass, set both flutes on the side of the spa, then slid forward, knees bent, so that his legs came around hers and her belly came into contact with his. Put his hands on her shoulders so he could look right into those eyes. 'You're a pleasure to be with, Emma Byrne.'

Emma stared into his warm brown eyes. She was going to pay for that pleasure sooner or later. This weekend had been one amazing adventure after another, one she'd re-member for ever.

'Hey, that's supposed to make you smile, not frown.'

'I'm not fr—'

'You are. You get that little line between your eye-brows...' He smoothed it away with a fingertip. 'Okay, I've got something guaranteed to make you smile.' His deep voice rumbled between them and he pressed closer, his burgeoning hardness hot and impatient against her belly.

'Mmm...'

'See? Smiling already.' He nipped his way up the side of her neck to the sensitive spot beneath her ear. 'How am I doing?' Tugged her earlobe between his lips, making her tingle.

'Pretty well.' His hands were a slippery delight on her shoulders.

'Only pretty well?'

She closed her eyes the better to savour it. Him. 'You can do better.'

A slow hand cruised down to her left breast to toy with her nipple. 'How about this?' He moved his mouth over hers and murmured, 'Is this good?'

'Mmm. Good.' *Very good.* She sighed and her lips opened under his probing tongue. It wasn't only his fabulously sexy body and his skill as a lover, it was their easy rapport, their shared interests.

Or was it something deeper?

Before she could ponder or react to that significant and scary thought he surged forward, his hands on either side of her face, his dark eyes holding hers. Slowly, slowly, he pushed that glorious hardness inside her. Slow and slippery and...oh, he was persuasive. Addictive.

'Tell me it's the best you ever had,' he demanded against her lips, withdrawing inch by excruciatingly exquisite inch, leaving her breathless and arching her hips in anticipation.

'Ha!' she managed. 'Isn't that what you guys all want to know?'

'Tell me you want more.' He leaned back just enough for her to see the wicked glint in his eyes and withdrew.

'Yes,' she moaned. 'More.' And moaned again as he pushed inside her, faster now, on a wild ride to paradise.

'Come with me.' His words sounded harsh and ragged against her ear as he came deep inside her.

'Coming,' she gasped as she rode over the edge of the velvet chasm with him.

Jake had chosen the room for its awesome view and the gas fire. The flames that licked over attractive smooth river stones provided warmth and intimacy. They sat in matching hotel robes on the rug in the flickering glow and shared the cold lobster and mango salad Room Service had delivered earlier.

He watched Emma slip a slice of mango between her lips. Tousled damp hair framed her face. Her eyes reflected the fire's orange glow, turning them violet and mysterious.

He wanted to know more of her secrets. More about the product line she'd developed and why she was so passionate about it that she'd spend so much of her free time immersed in it and yet not pursue its potential further.

Was it a front to hide behind? Was she lonely or a natural loner? Was she a risk-taker or not?

She was different to the women he usually got involved with. *So* different from the synthetic types to be found in King's Cross. Emma was sparkly and refreshing, a glint of dew on spring grass on a sunny morning. Her body was slender, firm, natural. Curves in all the right places and they were all real.

'Taste.' She swirled a sliver of lobster into the buttery sauce and held it to his lips. 'It's divine.'

He opened his mouth and let her feed him. Chewed a moment, savouring the flavour, the slight pressure of her finger against his lips.

The room's muted glow cast intimate shadows. 'Nothing beats romance, huh?'

She wiped her fingers on her napkin, her movements a

little jerky. Her eyes were still on his but rather than the dreamy violet from moments ago they were quicksilver-black. 'I don't do romance.'

The flat comment surprised him. 'No?' He waved an all-encompassing hand around the room—the flickering firelight on the walls, its warmth against his skin. 'What do you call this? The candlelit spa we just enjoyed?'

'Ambience.'

'So define romance.'

'Hearts and flowers and pretty words.' Silver sliced through her gaze, a knife's glint against ebony. 'I don't need them and I don't want them.'

'Why not?' He saw the pain in her eyes before she looked away. 'Surfer Boy wasn't the romantic type?'

She shrugged. 'That's just it. He was. Something special every Friday night and a dozen red roses every Wednesday, with a pretty note to say he was thinking of me...'

Her story didn't make sense to Jake. 'You weren't being totally honest with me about him the night of the dinner, were you?'

'Just because I don't want rom—'

'It's in your eyes. That's why you're not looking at me.'

'I'm...' Her shoulders drooped. 'Okay. I didn't slot him into my schedule. He slotted me into his. And I let him. Because, you see, I was stupidly in love with him.'

Jake reached out, trailed a finger down her cheek. 'He's even more of an idiot than I thought,' he murmured.

She shook her head. 'Romance is a lie to cover a lie.'

'It doesn't have to be, Emma.'

'No romance, okay? No lies.'

'Okay...' He pressed her down and rolled her onto her back on the rug, unknotting her belt and spreading her robe wide. 'Does that mean I can't tell you you're the sexiest woman I've ever made love to by firelight?'

She reached for his robe, pushing it away, fingers stretching and flexing over his shoulders, her eyes duelling with his, a smile on her lips and that little dimple in her cheek winking as he lowered himself on top of her. 'I'm okay with that.'

They had a late checkout on Monday morning so they spent it in bed and then enjoyed a quick lunch in a charming little rustic café before returning to Sydney. Emma had phoned in sick to work—something she'd never done before.

On the trip back she was almost tempted to open her laptop which Jake had returned to her, and catch up on the orders she'd neglected. But she knew she'd not be able to concentrate. Her mind was chock-full of distracting thoughts. So she watched the scenery flash by, and with it the slow return from fairytales and magical rides—of any kind—to civilisation and real life.

Real life. Depressing thought. Closing her eyes, she feigned sleep as they reached outer suburbia and let her mind drift back over the past two days.

She heard Jake speak on his mobile with his PA about some problem with a client that couldn't wait, enjoying the deep, authoritative timbre in his voice, remembering how it sounded when he came deep inside her.

Emma's phone signalled an incoming text. She considered ignoring it, but her responsible self wouldn't allow her to. She opened it and stared at the message. 'I don't believe it,' she murmured.

Jake glanced her way. 'Something wrong?'

'Mum's gone to Melbourne. With Stan.'

'Good for her.' Jake's voice was laced with a smile.

Emma texted back a reply before slipping her phone back into her bag. 'She's never done anything so impulsive in her life.'

'Then it's time she did.' With his eyes on the road, Jake put a hand on her thigh. 'Stan's a good guy. She'll be fine.'

'Of course she will.' She hoped. Because she wasn't looking forward to the fall-out if things went wrong.

'Your mum's a hard woman, Em,' he said, moments later. 'I know she was ill for a long time...'

'Clinical depression.' Emma hugged her arms, remembering the stress she and Stella had endured as a result. 'She's recovered now, but the after-effects linger on.' *And on.*

'Your dad's death caused it?'

She shook her head. 'She was depressed long before that. Dad didn't love her and there were other women.'

'Why didn't she just kick him out or walk away?'

'Because he had absolute control of her money. Remember, her generation isn't ours. And maybe she *wanted* to play the martyr.' The angst spilled out and it felt good. Really good. As if she was sweeping it out of her life. 'Just before Dad died he invested what was left of her inheritance and lost the lot.'

She heard Jake exhale loudly. 'That's tough, Emma. That's why you were always working?'

'I couldn't let the house be sold. It would've finished Mum off. Stella, being the nurturing soul she is, took on the role of carer.'

'So, forgive me if this offends you, why the hell does Bernice treat you the way she does? And why do you let her?'

A question Emma had asked herself often enough. 'Mum never appreciated the financial side of what I was doing—she just didn't see it. And Stella's been there for her in a more physical and emotional way.'

'So you erected a barrier to protect yourself from the rejection.'

'I guess I did. She doesn't get to me any more.'

He glanced at her. 'I disagree, Emma. It's still there.'

She shrugged—maybe he was right—and watched the glimpses of the ocean through the windscreen as they neared Coogee. 'She allowed my father to ruin her life. It spilled over to her daughters.'

And it reminded Emma why she wouldn't allow herself to think of what she and Jake had as anything more than a sexy encounter. She'd enjoyed it for what it was. But never again would she rely on anyone for her own happiness.

It felt odd, pulling up in her driveway in the middle of a work-day afternoon. She felt as if she'd lived a lifetime since she'd been home.

Jake switched off the engine, and the sudden silence in the car's confines seemed to shout. She busied herself searching her bag for her keys then realised she was already holding them.

She felt his gaze as he said, 'I guess you'll want to jump straight on your laptop and check out those orders that have piled up in your absence.'

His tone suggested that even if *she* wasn't down from the clouds and quite ready to settle to work just yet he was. He was probably used to switching from pleasure to business without a blink.

She fought down an absurd disappointment and turned with a smile fixed on her face. 'It doesn't go away, does it? Even when we do.'

He smiled back. 'Okay, then.' He pushed open the door and walked around to the boot to take out her belongings.

She took a careful, calming breath before climbing out and following him to the front door. She unlocked it and he ushered her past him and inside.

'Where do you want your gear?' he said behind her.

'Here's fine.' She gestured beside her and turned to him,

suddenly feeling like a stranger in her own surroundings. Everything felt different and she didn't know what to say. How ridiculous. She was experiencing morning-after awkwardness *now?*

He set the suitcase down and placed the garment bag on top, then straightened.

'Thanks.'

'No worries.'

She didn't know what to do with her hands and clasped them in front of her. How did you say goodbye to a man you'd just spent the past couple of nights having the best sex of your life with?

You said it casually, as if it happens all the time. 'Thanks for a great weekend.'

'My pleasure.' A flicker of heat darkened his gaze.

Mine too.

'I'll let you get to it, then.'

No *We'll have to do it again sometime.* 'Yes. Better get started. So...I'll see you...around.' God, did she sound needy? Clingy? Desperate?

He nodded, those dark eyes fixed on hers but giving nothing away. 'I'll give you a call some time.'

'Right.' Tomorrow? Next week? Next year?

He bent to kiss her. Just a brief brush of those expert lips over hers. Then he must have changed his mind because his arms slid around her waist and pulled her close. Her mouth opened beneath his and she let him in, tasting him as his tongue slid over hers. Her heart thudded against her chest and she clung to his shirt a moment before he lifted his head.

His eyes had changed, she noticed, like hot treacle. But she instinctively knew he wasn't going to act on it, so stepped back first. *At least maintain a little dignity.* 'Bye, then.'

'Catch you later.'

As he turned to leave his mobile buzzed and he yanked it out of his jacket pocket. 'Carmody.' He paused on Emma's doorstep, not looking at her while he listened to the caller. He didn't look back, walking into the sunshine, his attention already focused elsewhere.

Emma closed the door and listened to the purr of his car's engine as he drove off. She rubbed a hand over the familiar ache in her chest. It couldn't be love. Not again. She wouldn't let it be.

CHAPTER ELEVEN

EMMA found it tough going over the next couple of days at work—unable to concentrate, thinking of Jake, remembering their time together, wishing she could see him again even if it was just to remind herself that he was a one-weekend wonder. But she didn't hear from him.

Get over it. They'd had a fling. One wild, sexy weekend of pleasure. He'd never promised more. He'd been totally upfront with her. At least he'd been honest, and after Wayne that counted for a lot.

She felt different, though. Being with Jake had given her a new-found confidence in herself. As a woman, as a lover, as a person. She wanted to take on the world. She wanted to get serious about her business.

She wanted to see him so she could tell him that.

Meanwhile she filled her orders and surfed the internet for new soap-making recipes and considered how she might extend her client base.

On Thursday evening, humming along with her favourite jazz CD, she collected the ingredients together for honey soap. She melted glycerin bars and honey, poured it into a shallow pan, then melted the goat's milk, adding it to the mix. She'd just set it aside to cool when she heard the doorbell chime and went to answer it.

Jake.

He was leaning on her doorframe, reminding her of the last time she'd seen him standing there, and her heart tripped and she was breathless all over again. A burst of happiness sang through her veins as she met his warm brown eyes. Tonight he wore a luxurious-looking cream jumper over black trousers.

Her smile was spontaneous. 'Hi.'

'I was on my way out and passing this way...' The timbre of his deep, familiar voice turned her insides as hot and syrupy as the mix on her kitchen bench. 'Have I caught you at a bad time?'

'No...no.' She forced the surprise and excitement from her voice. *Act natural. He's on his way out, after all.* 'Come on in. I'm just finishing some soaps.' She turned, casting a deliberately casual glance over her shoulder as she moved to the kitchen. 'What brings you by?' When he didn't answer, she stopped at the kitchen table and turned. He almost crashed into her.

'You,' he said, his eyes melting into hers.

The heat from his body seemed to shimmer right through her. He smelled of warm wool and apple and cinnamon pie.

'More specifically, your soaps.' He rubbed his knuckles together audibly. 'It's my PA's birthday next week. I'd like to buy some for her.'

'Uh-huh. Well...' She swished her own hands down her coat. Her palms were sweating. 'I've got some pretty flower-shaped ones with a "Happy Birthday" imprint somewhere. I'll—'

'No birthday imprint.' He caught her arm as she started to move away.

'Oh. Okay...' She blinked once.

'She doesn't want anyone to know.' He lifted a shoulder. 'She's shy about birthdays.' Jake lowered his voice, curling his fingers around the lab coat's thick fabric. He felt Emma's gentle warmth beneath, the smooth muscle over bone against his palm, before letting his arm drop to his side. 'I thought I'd take some extras into the office at the same time. Let some of the staff try them out.'

'Really?' Surprise and humour glinted in her eyes and her lips curved and he knew she was wise to his game.

'Really.' He smiled back. 'What can you recommend?'

She moved to the plastic containers stacked along the wall. 'They're all made with goat's milk for sensitive skin, but I have a range of fragrances. How about amber, which has a sweet woody note suitable for both sexes? Or vanilla? Or, for something extra special…' She pulled out a container, carried it to the table. 'I've got some gorgeous little cupcake shapes in different fragrances—vanilla, blueberry, cinnamon, coconut. They're my favourite stock and very popular. I can pack them in a little basket for you if you want.'

He grinned. 'Do you wash with them or eat them?'

She opened the box, closed her eyes briefly and inhaled the fragrance, her ecstatic expression reminding him of when she'd come apart in his arms. She lifted out a pretty pink sample that matched the colour in her cheeks. 'I love cupcakes to death, but I wouldn't recommend eating these.'

Amazing, this transformation from the solemn girl who'd greeted him at her door only last week. The obvious joy she got from her creative work. The sparkle it put in her eyes and the glow it brought to her cheeks. And she was right; this was no mere hobby. Little wonder she'd been insulted he'd called it such. She had something unique here, a marketable product.

He leaned a hip against the table. 'Have you given any more thought to expanding this business online? Because

I see a different woman standing here tonight. One who might be willing to take that chance now.'

'Maybe I *am* a different woman.' He noticed her eyes had turned a darker hue as she looked at him. 'You've had something to do with that. And I *am* thinking about it.' She picked up a green cake, held it to his nose. 'What do you smell?'

'Fresh mown grass?'

'It gives a bathroom a pleasant scent.' She set it down. 'So many fragrances. I love them all.'

'Which one do you use?' He leaned in to catch more of that scent he'd missed over the past few days, heard her tiny intake of breath.

'Tahitian Fantasy.' Her breath hitched again. 'Why are you really here, Jake?'

Her husky voice vibrated against his lips as he set them on her smooth neck. 'Nothing like a little Tahitian Fantasy. Because I wanted to see you again. Are you okay with that?' His hands drifted to her waist, lips tracing a line over the fragrant flesh beneath her ear.

'Ah…yes…'

'Good, because I can't seem to stay away.' He nipped at her earlobe. 'What's in it?'

'The tiare flower. Tahitian gardenia.' She arched her neck. 'It has healing properties.'

'I've got this itch…'

'Where?' she murmured.

'Everywhere,' he murmured back, moving nearer, pressing open-mouthed kisses up her neck, over her jaw. 'I itch every damn where.'

'That sounds serious.' She stepped back to see his eyes, her own dancing as she slid his sleeve up to his elbow, fingers lightly massaging his forearm. 'Do you exfoliate?'

He had to lean forward so he could drop a lingering kiss on her lips. 'Only when I'm with you.'

Her blue eyes twinkled up at him. 'Ha-ha.' She picked up a dark-coloured soap that looked like congealed breakfast cereal. 'Honey and oatmeal,' she said, and gave his chest a light prod with one finger. 'Sit down...if you've got a moment?'

'For you, yes.' He yanked out a chair and watched her fill a shallow bowl with warm water.

The last time he'd been in her place she'd been uptight and defensive and prickly. Tonight she was the relaxed woman he'd enjoyed the weekend with.

Was it only four nights ago? It felt like four weeks. He'd spent those nights in a kind of limbo, caught between wanting to call and ask if he could come over and reminding himself they'd agreed on a weekend and the weekend was finished.

Had she spent the last few nights thinking of how good they'd been together? In bed and out of it? She was fresh, honest and fun to be with. He regretted putting a time limit on their affair.

'It's almost as good as sex.' Her words had him sitting up straighter as she carried the bowl to the table, set it in front of him along with a handtowel.

'What is?'

'Push up your sleeves and put your hands in the bowl.' She moistened the soap in the water and worked it between her palms till it glistened, then slid it over and around his hand in a slow, slippery massage. 'Good?'

He watched, fascinated, her small fingers with their short neat nails gliding over his, between his. He looked up, met her eyes. 'Very good. Exceptionally good. But... Do I need to work on my bedroom technique?'

The twinkle in her eyes sharpened. Her lips stretched

into a full-on smile. 'Okay, that was my selling point before the weekend. Damn—now I'll have to think of something else.'

'We could always test the theory again, just to be sure...'

'There's nothing wrong with your technique, Jake.' She twined her fingers against his. Silky heat on silky heat.

'Nor yours.' He reciprocated, pressing his thumb into her palm and drawing lazy circles, watching her cheeks pinken, her eyes turn to liquid pools of blue desire.

His own vision was growing hazy as they continued to watch each other while they made out with their joined hands. 'Do you give all your clients the personal treatment?'

She leaned in so that her lips were a whisper away from his. 'Only the ones who knock on my door.'

'I've been thinking,' he murmured back, 'there's no reason why we can't continue seeing each other, is there?'

Her whole body stilled. 'What are you saying?'

He soothed his lips over hers just once. 'I like being with you. Don't look too far ahead. Let's just enjoy the ride. What do you say?'

'Uh-huh...'

He lifted her damp fingers to his mouth, kissed them and released her. 'In the meantime, I've got an appointment in King's Cross. If tonight goes as planned, tomorrow the Pink Mango could be looking at a new owner.'

She continued to stare at him, unblinking, gaze unfocused. 'Uh-huh.'

But she didn't seem to hear him. 'Don't congratulate me yet,' he said anyway. He wiped his hands on her little towel, then pushed up. 'Talk to you tomorrow evening.'

'Uh-huh.'

He folded the towel, set it on the table. 'I'll let myself out.'

He smiled to himself when he heard her call, 'Yes!' as clear as crystal as he walked to the door.

For Emma, the following work day dragged. Unlike what was happening with Jake, which seemed to be taking off at warp speed. She couldn't focus on anything except their unexpected sexy interlude last night.

He liked being with her. He wanted to be with her some more. It brought a smile to her lips every time she remembered. So often that her co-workers cast more than a few Emma-had-got-lucky glances her way over the course of the day.

She left the call centre five minutes before closing time; something she'd never done before. She tapped along with the beat of the latest pop song on the radio as she drove home, looking forward to Jake's call.

It was nearly six o'clock when he rang. Emma picked the phone up on its first ring.

'It's done,' he said without preamble. 'The Pink Mango's history.'

She almost heard the drum-roll of satisfaction in his voice and smiled. 'Hooray for you.'

'Can you clear your evening schedule and come out to celebrate with me?'

Her smile broadened. 'Consider it cleared.'

'I'll pick you up in thirty minutes?'

'*Thirty* minutes?'

'You'll look gorgeous whatever you're wearing,' he said, obviously familiar with the female ritual, 'and I've got somewhere casual in mind.'

Thirty-five minutes later, after three changes of clothes, she'd decided on her best jeans and an ivory jumper with a bright turquoise-and-orange scarf when he arrived.

Seeing him was like cresting the top of a rollercoaster

wave, all excitement and anticipation. He wore black jeans and a black T-shirt beneath an often washed black, white and navy flannel shirt, open down the front. Definitely casual.

'Hi.' She sounded as breathless as she felt.

'Hi.' With one arm still propped against the doorframe he tugged on her scarf, pulled her towards him and kissed her.

He tasted *sooo* good, and she felt herself rushing down the other side of that slippery breaker. Then he straightened, and with a wickedly hot twinkle in his eyes, said, 'If we don't get moving we might never get there.'

'Wait up. You forgot something last night.' She picked up a little cellophane-wrapped basket from the shelf by the door and held it out with a grin. 'Tell your PA happy birthday from me.'

He nodded, eyes twinkling. 'How much do I owe you?'

'Nothing. Free sample.'

'Are you sure?'

'Positive. Promotion's good for business.'

'Okay, but don't forget to write it off as an expense.'

Moments later they were cruising along a well-lit Bondi street bustling with Friday-night shoppers. But Jake bypassed the usual restaurants and turned into a suburban street.

She looked out at the luxury homes, roofs glinting in the streetlights. 'Where are we going?'

He pulled up in front of a buttercream wall. Beyond, Emma could see an expansive red-tiled roof. 'Welcome to Jake's Place. Home of great food and magnificent views.' He pressed a remote and the gates swung open revealing a large two-storey house.

'Wow.' She took in the view as the car came to a stop under an open carport. A long curve of beach, dark now but for a couple of lights blinking near the horizon. 'It's magnificent, Jake. You've achieved so much in such a short time.' The location alone had to be worth a fortune.

He swiped the keys from the ignition, his gaze on the black waves laced with a fine line of white in the distance. 'The bank still has a share, but we're getting there.'

Reaching across the console between them, he cupped the back of her neck with one hand, unclipped her seat belt with the other, his gaze hot with smouldering promise. And before she could blink he meshed his lips with hers.

He'd had no intention of jumping her until he'd fed her, but when Jake looked into those sapphire eyes which had kept him from the precious little sleep he'd managed over the past few nights, every thought flew out of his mind bar one. Having Emma.

'Have you missed me?' he murmured against her lips. When had he ever asked that question? he wondered vaguely, and was stupidly happy when he felt her lips curve against his mouth.

'Yes.' She sucked in a breath.

His impatient fingers found the hem of her jumper and rushed beneath to feel the firm, warm flesh of her torso, the ridges along her ribcage, and higher to the curve under her breasts. Her nipples tightened as he swirled his fingers over the crests. Beneath his hands he felt the same urgency that whipped through his own body as she strained against his palm.

'Emma...' The breathless sound registered somewhere as his own voice. 'Missed you too.' Flicking the clasp, he loosened her bra, shoved it up and out of the way so he could feast on the sweet taste of an engorged nipple. He slid his palm between her thighs, cupped her hard through the hot denim, felt her shudder and arch in response, heard her muffled sigh as she forked her fingers through his hair and pulled it tight against his scalp.

He heard a rushing noise in his ears; it might have been the sea, or her ragged breath, or the fizz of his own blood. All he knew was if he didn't get out now he'd have her here, in the car, before sanity could prevail.

Swearing and fumbling with the latch, he pushed the passenger door open. Somehow they were both out of the car and stumbling together towards the house.

His keys… In the car—somewhere. The hell with them. He had her up against the wall, mouths fused, teeth clashing, his raging erection pressing into the soft give of her belly before either of them knew what had happened.

Did she have any idea how much power she wielded over him? He never lost it like this. Her pupils were dark and dilated when he lifted his head to watch her while he snapped open the top button of her jeans.

She returned the favour, hard little knuckles against his belly as she loosened the stud.

There was a harsh zipping sound as they freed each other. And then he was lifting her against the wall and pushing into her familiar sultry heat, his tongue mimicking the action as it dived inside her mouth to drown in her taste.

Fast, furious, frantic. No time to think. Just blind, burning lust, passion and pleasure. She seemed to struggle for air, and he lifted his lips, as breathless as she, and watched her, head thrown back, neck pale and slender in the cool wash of light angling in from the street.

Then his mouth was there, on that galloping pulse, her smooth fragrant skin. Exquisite taste. Pure sensuality.

But the need she conjured in him as he rode the wave to completion, this desperation, as if she was tearing something from deep within him, was beyond his experience.

Moments later, his body still humming, he lowered her to her feet, rested his brow against hers. 'What is it with you? I can't seem to get enough—'

Protection. He froze. He'd not given it a thought. Not given Emma's welfare or safety a thought. What kind of man did that make him? He lifted her chin with a finger and stared into her eyes. 'We just had unprotected sex, Emma.'

'We didn't use a condom, no.' She didn't look fazed or alarmed. Her eyes were clear and calm, like the sea on a summer day.

'I...if anything happens...'

'It won't. I'm still on the pill.'

He relaxed a little. 'You didn't tell me.'

'You didn't ask.' She lifted a shoulder, then wiggled back into her jeans. 'And I wasn't as sure about you then...'

He caught her drift. 'I'm healthy, Emma.'

If they'd been in full light he'd have sworn her eyes darkened, and she rolled her lips together in that way she had before saying, 'I wanted *you* inside me, not a piece of rubber.'

Her words hit hard, right where his heart suddenly pounded like a hammer on steel. His fingers tightened as he adjusted his own clothing. 'I should've been more careful. I always use condoms.' Just not this time.

'I take care of my own protection,' she said.

Emma didn't want to talk about it. Not another word. *Oh, no.* Her heart suddenly cramped, twisted as she realised the full import of what she'd just admitted. She'd wanted that closer connection with him. Craved it like an addict. *Dangerous.* Had she made the right decision to continue seeing Jake after all?

She rubbed a hand over her chest. 'It's cold out here,' she said, hugging her arms. 'Can we go inside?'

He mumbled something about keys and walked to the car, fishing around in the luxury interior a moment before coming back, keys in hand. 'Come on—you can take a look around while I cook.'

She used the time alone to refocus her thoughts while she explored Jake's domain. The décor was essentially masculine but comfortable. Lots of glass, dark furniture with splashes of colour—maroon, grey, red. The wood-panelled kitchen was surprisingly clean and tidy, putting hers to shame. But then, he had enough cupboard space and mod cons for the both of them. An office with two computers and three monitors, and a fortune in the latest technology in the living room.

The upstairs bedrooms were mostly empty except for Jake's. A massive king-size bed dominated the room with its tan and navy quilt and minimal furniture. She backed away from the reminder that other women had no doubt enjoyed themselves there and hurried downstairs.

He'd slapped a couple of thick steaks on the grill and was slicing an avocado when she returned to the kitchen, but he waved away her offer of help so she wandered to the living room. Windchimes filled the balcony beyond the floor-to-ceiling windows, the sound tinkling and clacking in the gentle breeze. Solar-powered balls of crackled glass slowly spun multi-coloured lights over the deck.

He appeared moments later with the aromatic steaks, a bowl of healthy-looking salad and a loaf of crusty bread.

They ate while a blues CD poured music out of the speakers with only the solar-powered balls for lighting—'ambience', he was quick to point out—and washed it down with a nice cabernet sauvignon while they watched a passenger ship track north, myriad tiny lights blazing.

He topped up her glass. 'What's the latest on your mum?'

'She's still in Melbourne. Staying in Stan's house, of all places. *And* she's still deciding when she'll come home.'

'Having a new man in her life's obviously done her good.' He grinned. 'Maybe she'll be a little more mellow on her return.'

'Maybe.' It helped that Jake understood, and Emma was glad she'd opened up on that topic; it felt good to share.

He rose, collected their plates. 'Why don't you go make yourself comfortable on the couch and I'll make coffee? What's your preference?'

'Cappuccino, please. With extra chocolate?'

While he attended to the coffee machine she walked out onto the deck to feel the salt breeze and hear the sound of the sea. She told herself that she was right where she wanted to be. With a guy whose company she enjoyed. She refused to let herself think beyond the ride he'd promised.

When she walked inside he'd brought the coffee and a bowl of dark chocolates and she snuggled against him on the couch. She listened to his heart beating strong and solid against her ear, the fresh fragrance of sun-dried clothes and his clean scent in her nostrils. He turned on the TV. Some old adventure movie was playing. She tuned out, closed her eyes, and moments later felt herself drifting...

'You're tired,' he murmured. 'Stay the night.'

The spell she was falling under shattered like glass. She kept her eyes closed but her mind was instantly alert. Unlike their fantasy weekend in paradise, this was the real world. And in the real world she was...falling in love with this man.

Even as the words formed in her mind she was shoving them away, squeezing them out of her heart. She refused, *refused* to fall in love again. She'd been there, done that, and had the scars to prove it. Her mother had fallen for a man who'd not loved her and it had brought nothing but pain and misery to herself, her husband and her daughters—even long after he'd died.

'You're thinking too hard again.' He curled a hand around her head and stroked her hair. 'You won't need pyjamas, and I've got a spare toothbrush.'

Oh, yes, she'd bet he did.

'So...spend the night with me?'

She opened her eyes, looked into his and felt her heart tumble further. 'I can't,' she all but whispered.

A puzzled crease formed between his brows. 'I'll drive you back in plenty of time in the morning. I can even wait while you get your swimsuit and drop you off at the beach if you want.'

'We'll see each other, Jake, but I won't be staying nights.'

A beat of silence. 'I'm not Wayne, Emma,' he said quietly.

'I know. I just need my space for a bit. This is all happening too fast.' She couldn't help it. She reached up, touched his clean-shaven jaw. 'Okay?'

'Okay. I won't pressure you. It's too soon. I get that. But if you change your mind...'

She nodded, feeling the strength drain out of her. 'Thanks. But you're right. I'm tired and, if it's okay with you, I'd like to go home now.'

He exhaled a slow, deep breath, then pushed off the couch. 'I'll get my keys.'

When a woman didn't want to spend the night with him, he... He what? Jake frowned at his darkened ceiling later that night. He couldn't remember the last time.

He swung out of bed, dragged on old shorts, T-shirt and sneakers, then headed downstairs and out into the salty night air. The chill spattered his skin with goosebumps as he made his way along a couple of streets to the beach. Black waves surged and thumped on the sand as he jogged off the road and onto the esplanade.

She had good reasons, he reminded himself, and it wasn't personal—the scumbag surfer had done a real number on her.

He'd respect her space, give her time. That fragile heart of hers was still healing, and no way was he going to be responsible for further damage. Meanwhile they could continue to enjoy what they *did* have, keeping it casual.

A car skidded to a stop a short distance away, drawing his attention. The back door swung open, something flopped onto the road and the vehicle sped off. What the...? Switching direction to the way he'd come, he increased his pace.

The small bundle of dirty fur moved, and two frightened eyes looked up at his. Jake's heart melted. 'Hey, fella. Steady.' He looked the dog over, murmuring soothing noises. No ID. Beneath the matted white fur he was skin and bone, and alive with fleas. Abandoned in the middle of the night. Poor little scrap.

'Come on, Scratch. We'll find you some place safe.' Sliding a finger beneath the grimy collar, he picked the little guy up and set off for home. In a different life he'd have kept him, but he had no choice but to hand him to the nearest animal shelter first thing.

With Scratch contained in the laundry, with a bowl of water, a left-over sausage and an old cushion to sleep on, Jake's thoughts turned to Emma again as he climbed the stairs to snatch a couple of hours of sleep.

She was sexy, had a sense of humour, and was good company in and out of bed. If she wouldn't stay the night he'd accept that. Because she was Emma. She wasn't only a lover, she was a friend. There was something so easy about being with her, and she brought more to his life on so many levels than any woman ever had.

Careful, mate. He was starting to sound like Ry. *Hell.* He flopped backwards onto his bed. That was one very dangerous thought.

CHAPTER TWELVE

THE sea was as calm as glass on Sunday morning, but the air chilled Emma's body as she waded in for her morning workout. The sun had lifted out of the ocean, spreading crimson and gold across the sky.

Sliding beneath the surface, she kept close to the shoreline between the red and yellow safety flags, swimming hard until her limbs warmed and softened. She trod water, watching the sun glimmer on the surface, and waved to a regular fellow swimmer before heading back the other way.

Jake had come by yesterday evening, late and tired. Working his day job and dealing with the sale of the club would take a toll on anyone. She'd made popcorn on one occasion and they'd made love—on every occasion. On the couch. In her tiny shower stall. In her too-small bed. But he hadn't stayed. She'd been unable to sleep for the rest of the night, knowing there was a big warm man in a big warm bed a few kilometres away who'd have been happy to share.

She headed for her towel farther up the beach. Sunday mornings brought out tourists and locals alike. Walking up the shallow steps towards the lawns bordering the esplanade, she watched a group of families set up for a picnic breakfast.

Only now, with Jake in her life, was she realising how isolated she'd let herself become over the years. She needed to make an effort to go out and socialise more.

She wrung out her hair, tied it into a high ponytail, then changed into her track suit in the change rooms, dumping her swimsuit and towel into her hold-all.

On such a beautiful day she didn't want to go home and deal with business, shut away from people and life. She'd splash out on a take-away hot chocolate on the way home. She might even add a cake to her order and sit at an outdoor table on Coogee Beach Road and people-watch awhile.

A big guy with a black-and-white dog on a leash was approaching when she reached the traffic lights. He waved and she pushed up her sunglasses. Jake? With a dog?

She waved back, and suddenly that sunshine seemed a whole lot warmer. The whole world seemed that much brighter. He was looking at her as if he wanted to eat her while he waited for the lights to change.

He crossed the road and kissed her right there on the footpath. 'Hello, gorgeous girl,' he said when he let her up for air. 'Mmm—salt.'

She licked his familiar taste from her lips. 'I wonder why.' He was a beautiful sight, even in a ratty T-shirt smudged with what looked suspiciously like doggy paw prints. She bent to pat the gorgeous black-and-white pooch of indeterminate pedigree at his feet. 'I didn't know you had a dog.'

'He's not mine, unfortunately. I walk him for an elderly neighbour who can't get out much these days. Say hello to Seeker.' He patted the dog's head. 'Shake hands, boy.'

At Jake's command, Seeker sat down and lifted a paw, big puppy eyes looking up at her and a doggy smile as wide as the beach. 'Oh, aren't you *gorgeous?*' She squatted down to ruffle his well maintained fur and was rewarded with a sloppy kiss. 'I always, always wanted a dog, but Mum said no.' *And hadn't she decided her perfect man in her perfect world would love animals?*

'I still do, but these days with my lifestyle it wouldn't be fair, so I get my animal fix with Seeker, here. Some people don't deserve pets.' He frowned. 'I had to turn an abandoned dog in to a shelter yesterday.'

'That's so sad—not to mention criminal. If you can't give a pet the time and love it deserves, don't have one. I'm going for hot chocolate. Would you like to join me? We can get take-away and walk if you like.'

His grin was one-hundred-percent contagious. 'I would. I didn't stop for breakfast. Had to give Seeker his doggy bath.'

'You groom him too?'

'It's part of the fun. He's all mine every Sunday morning unless I'm out of town. There's a dog-friendly park a ten-minute walk away. I can let Seeker off the leash. I've got his *B-A*-double-*L*.'

She laughed. 'He's gorgeous *and* smart.'

Like you, Jake thought, watching her bury her face in fur.

'So how come I've never seen you down here before?' she said, straightening.

'I don't usually come this far. I was on my way to see you, as a matter of fact. Good timing—I was hoping to catch you on your way home from the beach. If not I was going to hunt you down at your place and interrupt you.'

'Oh? Why?'

Because I can't get you out of my mind. I want to be with you all the damn time. 'Can't a guy see his favourite girl?'

She blushed, and her smile was the best thing he'd seen

all morning. 'I thought you said you were going in to the club today.'

'I am. Later.' He'd delayed his meeting with the buyer by a couple of hours—something he'd never have done for any other woman. He slung an arm around her shoulders with an unnerving feeling that with Emma he was swimming in uncharted waters. 'But here you are, so let's get that breakfast you promised and take it to the park.'

'*I* promised?' She smiled up at him, the light in her eyes reflecting the sun's sparkle off the sea. 'I never promised breakfast.'

'Okay, you buy the hot chocolate; I'll spring for the rest.'

They took their purchases to the park: two hot chocolates and a couple of cupcakes drizzled with icing. They shared half a soggy bacon and egg burger with wilting lettuce and mayonnaise, and let Seeker snaffle the other half.

After a vigorous game of chase-the-ball, which Emma threw herself into with enthusiasm, Jake suggested they walk back to his place, return Seeker on the way, and he'd drive her home on his way to the club.

They headed towards Bondi. Emma jogged a few steps ahead with Seeker, chasing a white butterfly, her slim figure as watch-worthy as any catwalk model, her ponytail bouncing and swinging in time with her steps.

They'd been lovers just over a week. With a little of the edge gone after those first frenzied encounters he'd expected the attraction to fade somewhat, as it invariably did. It hadn't. They'd had fun this morning. She'd not fussed over her sea-damp hair and lack of make-up like other women he dated would. Her tracksuit was smeared with paw-prints and covered in fur.

He'd never in a million years considered asking a

woman to come out and play ball with a dog in a park on a Sunday morning. With Emma it came naturally.

'Hope you weren't worried,' he said when they reached Mrs G's front door.

'Of course not, Jake.' The white-haired lady turned her smile on Emma. 'And you found your friend.'

'Mrs G, I'd like you to meet Emma. Emma, this is Grace Goodman—everyone calls her Mrs G.'

'Pleased to meet you, Emma. Jake was hoping to run into you.'

Emma smiled up at him, then at Grace. 'Nice to meet you too. We've had a lovely morning.'

'I don't how I'd manage without this young man here,' Mrs G told Emma. 'He's taken good care of both of us since my Bernie died. I broke my hip last year, and I can't get out like I used to.'

'Afraid I can't stay,' he said, with an apology in his grin and handing the leash to Mrs G. 'Got work.'

Grace shook her head. 'You work too hard. You and this lovely girl here should be out enjoying yourselves.'

Emma smiled at him. 'Work comes first.'

He knew Emma understood. She believed it as much as he—something some of his other lovers hadn't. But he was also working on the playtime her life had been lacking. The idea of convincing Emma to let him take the rest of the day off with her was tempting, but he had to meet the new club owner and go over the books.

They farewelled Mrs G, then picked up his car. He dropped Emma home first. But he lingered over a long hot kiss before letting her go. 'See you tonight.'

On Tuesday Emma had a rostered day off—and her first luncheon date with Jake.

Since Jake had clients all morning, she was meeting

him at his office. His *real* office, which he shared with
two other professionals. In a respectable building in the
commercial heart of the city.

She rode the elevator to the fourteenth floor, smoothed
the lapel on her black jacket as she stepped into a bright
reception area with wide windows and glimpses of the
Harbour Bridge between the skyscrapers. A dark-haired
woman with exotic eyes that hinted at her Asian heritage
greeted her with a professional smile at the desk. So different from the first time she'd met him at his place of
work—and in so many ways.

Emma smiled back. 'I'm Emma Byrne and I'm here to
see Jake Carmody.'

'Oh. Emma, hello.' Her professional smile widened to
friendly interest. 'I'm Jasmine. Jake told me to expect you.
He's with someone at the moment. Can I get you a coffee
or something while you wait?'

'Thanks, I'm fine.'

'And thank you for sending in the soaps. They're a real
hit. I'm making a list of people wanting to buy more.'

'That's very kind of you.'

'Are you sure I can't get you a coffee?'

She shook her head, smiling back. 'I'll just admire the
view.'

'It's not nearly as spectacular as where you're going for
lunch. I booked the table.' She lowered her voice to a con-
spiratorial whisper. 'Oh, and I probably wasn't supposed
to tell you that.'

Emma had expected to grab something in the little café
downstairs, and was pleasantly surprised. 'I didn't hear a
thing.'

'Don't plan on getting any work done for the rest of the
afternoon. I— Excuse me a moment,' she said when the
phone rang. 'Carmody and Associates.'

Ten minutes later Jasmine was still handling what seemed to be a complex call. Emma glanced at her watch and flicked through another magazine. Maybe they should postpone their lunch for another time. He was obviously busy.

Even as she considered it, she heard a door open and Jake's voice in the corridor. '...Any time—and don't worry. It's all going to be fine.'

'Thank you, Jake,' a woman's voice said. 'For everything.' Her voice trembled. 'You've given me a chance to start over and I'll never forget it.'

'Just put it all out of your mind for now, and concentrate on spending some quality time with Kevin while I get things rolling.'

The woman appeared first, in jeans a size too big on her too-thin frame and a faded black top slipping off one shoulder. Her hair was scooped into a knot on top of her head and she carried a thumb-sucking toddler on her hip.

Familiar...Emma racked her brain, trying to place her as Jake followed close behind. He walked the woman to the elevators on the other side of Reception, squeezed the woman's bony shoulders as she entered the lift.

Then Emma remembered where she'd seen her. The waitress from the Pink Mango. Cherry.

Obviously a woman like her couldn't afford to be paying Jake for his professional services, yet he was treating her with the care and respect he'd offer any fee-paying client.

Then he turned and saw her, and his frown cleared and his face lit up. 'Emma. Sorry to keep you waiting. Unexpected delay. Hang on a sec, I have something for you.' He disappeared again into his office.

Jasmine, still on the phone, smiled at Emma and rolled her eyes as she spoke to the caller.

Then Jake returned with a fluffy black-and-white stuffed dog. 'According to the tag, his name's Fergus.'

'Oh...' A warm squishy feeling spread through her body. 'You got me a dog.'

'I hope you like stuffed animals.'

'I did, I do. I guess I never grew up.' She'd mentioned never having pets and he'd bought her the next best thing. 'Thank you.'

He jerked a thumb at the busy Jasmine to indicate they were off, then walked Emma to the elevator. It was crowded with office workers headed out for lunch. He flagged down a cab, then they took a short ride to the Centre Point Tower.

She stared up at the famous landmark, as high as the Eiffel Tower. 'We're going up there?'

'I know you hate heights, but I'm sure you'll enjoy the food,' he said as they shuffled towards one of the elevators that shot sightseers to the observation deck, the Skywalk and other adventures Emma had never felt the urge to discover. 'Don't look till we're there.'

She slipped her hand in his and looked up at him. 'Maybe it's time I did.' Steeling her stomach muscles for the inevitable drop, she let out a nervous laugh. 'I might even surprise myself and enjoy it.'

And she didn't shut her eyes once all the way to the top—which seemed to take for ever. The three-hundred-and-sixty-degree revolving restaurant afforded magnificent views of Botany Bay and as far away as the Blue Mountains. She was so proud of herself she even ventured to the slanted window for a quick dizzying glimpse to the street way below.

Jake's hand on her shoulder and his 'Congratulations' made it even more special. She might never have had the nerve to try if he hadn't been there to encourage her. But her legs were still shaky as she set Fergus on the edge of the table.

Jake ordered white wine and a shared seafood platter for starters. He'd made the right decision about the venue—seeing the almost shy pleasure in Emma's eyes when she'd faced her natural fear was worth it.

'Any other plans for your day off?' he asked, setting the menu aside.

'I have an appointment with a potential client at two-thirty.'

'New client?' He leaned forward, interested. 'That's great, Em. Where?'

'It's a new natural products shop in the mall where I work.'

'So we've plenty of time.' He raised his glass. 'Cheers.'

'Cheers.' She tapped her glass to his.

'Emma, I've been thinking about you getting your products out there. Letting people sample them. Why don't you ask one of the shops you supply if you can set up a display one Saturday morning or during late-night shopping hours? I'll give you a hand. You might sound out this place this afternoon, since they're new, and see if they're interested.'

The seafood platter arrived and she selected a prawn. 'That's an idea.'

'We'll need to set up a website first, in case customers ask, and get some business cards printed so they can contact you.'

'You really think my products are good enough for all that hoopla?'

'Hoopla?' Had no one ever encouraged her to aim for the stars? 'Are you kidding? After that sensual demonstration the other night?' He pointed the crab claw he was holding her way. 'You'll never know if you don't give it a

go. Honey, have a little faith. In yourself *and* your products.'

'I'm trying to. I *do*,' she corrected, and gave a half-
laugh. 'Force of habit. I'm not used to others sharing my
enthusiasm, and I'm still getting accustomed to the different mind-set.' Setting her palms on the table, she leaned
forward with a grin. 'Of *course* you have confidence in
my products; why wouldn't you? They're the best you ever
tried, right?'

'Right.' He grinned back. 'We'll make a start tonight,'
he decided. 'I'll come over when you get home and we'll
make plans.'

Emma took another sip of cool fruity wine while she
thought about his ideas. She didn't want to let him—or
herself—down, especially when he was so busy. Surely
she could try it on her own? Even if she just let him help
her with the IT side of things? 'You're very generous with
your time, Jake. As if you haven't got enough to do with
your practice and winding up the club. Are you sure?'

'Of course I'm sure. I want to help you any way I can.'

'Cherry obviously thinks you're pretty wonderful too.'

He looked slightly stunned. 'You know Cherry?'

'I recognised her from the club. I didn't know she had
a child, though. I guess you don't think of people in that
industry as being mums and having otherwise ordinary
lives. She looked pretty down...' She waved a hand. 'Sorry,
it's none of my business.'

'Cherry and her kid were evicted from their accommodation a couple of weeks ago. She came to me for help.'

Emma understood that feeling, that desperation, all too
well. She'd had to work after school to help pay the bills
when her mum had been too depressed to get out of bed for
weeks on end. 'That's a horrible, gut-wrenching feeling,

and even worse with the added responsibility of a child. What about women's shelters?'

'Do you have any idea how many homeless people there are in Sydney?' His expression changed, and his eyes met hers with an understanding she'd not expected. 'Maybe you do.'

Emma nodded. 'It wasn't that desperate with us, but it so easily could have been. So Cherry came to you?' She remembered the woman's tremulous and relieved voice outside Jake's office. Cherry saw the kind of man Emma saw. An approachable man, an honest man, someone she could trust to help her and her child in a time of desperate need. A man who was generous with his time and expertise. 'It shows how highly she thinks of you.'

But he shook his head as if it was nothing. 'She needed a place for the night, for herself and Kevin. I told her there was a room at the back of the club she could use until we sorted something out. She's staying there for the time being.'

'If anyone can help it'll be Jake Carmody.'

They didn't talk for a moment while they sampled more of the delicious food. 'So...who looks after Kevin when Cherry's working?' Emma asked between mouthfuls.

Jake chose a prawn, peeling it carefully while he answered. 'The girls take shifts. They're a tight bunch. Protective. Mostly they're just people trying to make a living the best and sometimes the only way they know how.'

Emma didn't miss the slightly defensive tone. As if he had a personal interest or understanding. She speared a piece of pickled octopus. 'So what happens next? Obviously that can't work for ever.'

'I've bought a place. It needs some work, but I'm using the sale of the club to finance it. Temporary accommodation for people like Cherry to stay until they get themselves on their feet. I've asked Cherry if she'll run it. It'll get her out of the club scene.'

She took a moment to consider his words before she answered. He seemed so sure—as if he'd thought this through over a long period of time. 'This is very important to you.'

Jake nodded, selecting another crab claw, snapping it open. Damn right it was. It was the only good thing to come out of his inheritance: an ability to make a change for the better. If he only helped one person it would be worth it.

'I've been around that strip club for a big chunk of my life, Emma. Seeing women and their kids come and go. Seeing their lack of power over their own circumstances, the hopelessness in their eyes. Wanting to do something to break the cycle. That's why I went into law. I may not have had the world's best upbringing, but I've turned it around, I think.'

He saw her shift closer, elbows on the white tablecloth, her fresh, clean fragrance wafting towards him. 'I reckon you have,' she said softly. 'You should be careful, Jake, a girl could fall hard for a guy like you.'

His head shot up. Her eyes… Maybe, just *maybe,* there was a hint of those for ever stars in that blue sparkle? He shredded another prawn while his heart tumbled strangely. 'Not a girl like you, Emma. You're too smart.'

The little crease dug between her brows as she popped an olive in her mouth. 'Why not a girl like me?'

Careful. The last thing Emma needed right now was another crack in that heart. 'We're both career types, you and me,' he said, avoiding her gaze. 'Work hard, play hard.'

But were good times all he really had in common with

Emma? He'd never discussed the club or his upbringing or his reasons for his choice of career with anyone. Not even Ryan. Though his mate knew of his father's business they'd never talked about it. Yet he'd talked about it with Emma. But she didn't need to know his whole life history.

Shaking the thoughts away, he lifted his glass, drained his wine, then said, 'Tell me more about this shop you've discovered that's going to help send your new career soaring...'

Emma drove home, her mind abuzz. The new shop was happy for her to promote her products with a display—this coming Friday evening, no less, to coincide with their first week of trading.

Jake was the only one who'd ever shown an interest and inspired her to take the plunge. Jake's encouragement and support had lifted her spirits and caught her enthusiasm. With his help she might just be able to make it work. Correction: she *would* make it work.

With his help so many people were better off, she thought. She thought too, how he'd chosen a career so he could help people like Cherry—the girls and their plights had made a lasting impression on him.

Because he'd grown up around the strip club. For how long? she wondered. Had his mother been a stripper? How long had it been since he'd seen her? She remembered the fleeting expression in his eyes when he'd spoken of her, just once, on the night of the hens' party—at odds with the casual indifference in his voice.

She hadn't let herself become interested in his past because what they had was based around the present. But now she simply couldn't ignore it. His past had shaped him into the man he was. He might be fun-loving, casual and outgoing but there were shadows there too.

She switched direction and headed for his place. There was so much more she wanted to know.

CHAPTER THIRTEEN

EMMA pressed the intercom on the wall outside Jake's home. 'It's me,' she said, when he answered. 'Let me in.'

The gate slid open and by the time she'd reached the door Jake was waiting for her, naked but for a towel low around his hips. 'I thought we arranged to meet at your place, but if you've come to share my shower...' His sexy grin faded when he realised she wasn't smiling back. 'Something wrong? Didn't it work out with the new clients?'

'No, no, nothing like that. It went well, really well, and I'll tell you about it later. But...' She waved a hand. 'Can we talk?'

He gestured her inside. 'Let's go to the living room.'

She followed him, then went to the window and looked out at the sea while she took a calming breath. She didn't know how it was going to go. Whether he'd resent her for what he might see as an intrusion on his privacy. But this was too important to ignore.

'I've been thinking about what you said this afternoon,' she said slowly. 'About Cherry and the place you've bought. How important it is to you.'

'It is, yes. Is that a problem for you?'

'Of course not.' She turned to face him. 'But why buy

a place? Why be personally involved? Why not give to a homeless charity instead? *Why* is it so important?'

Jake listened to her rapid-fire questions while he dragged in a slow, slow breath. Having Emma come into his life was one of the most life-changing events he'd ever experienced. To his surprise, he discovered he wanted to answer them, to have her listen and understand. His only concern was if once he started he might not be able to stop.

He crossed the room, gripped her shoulders loosely and steered her towards the couch. 'Sit down.' He sat down beside her, fisted his hands on his thighs. Took another breath. 'I lived there, Emma. The back of that strip club was home sweet home. So I know first-hand what it's like to be powerless.'

'Oh…Jake.' She lifted a hand, thought better of it and drew it back. 'How long?'

He shifted a shoulder, always uncomfortable with sympathy. But that wasn't what she was offering. Just support and a willingness to listen with an open mind. He'd never realised he'd needed it until now.

He gazed through the windows into the deepening twilight. 'I was five when Mum left in the middle of the night. I hadn't started school yet. I had no friends. Can't blame her, Earl cheated on her as regular as clockwork. She worked late-night shifts cleaning offices, so I saw all sorts come and go at our apartment. One night she just didn't come home. It was like losing an arm.' Or a heart.

Emma didn't speak, but he felt her reaching out to him with streamers of warmth that touched the dark, secret places inside him.

'It was lonely and isolating—after all, I could hardly ask schoolmates to come over and play. As I grew up I understood what had happened, and I swore I'd never be like *him*.' His fists tightened against his thighs. 'But the one person I'd counted on, the one person I'd loved and trusted, left me there. She didn't take me with her and it hurt like hell.'

He felt her hands cover his fists and looked into her moisture-sheened eyes.

'Your mum stayed in a loveless marriage, Emma, but she stayed. Even a mum who gives you grief is better than no mum at all—at least yours had some compassion, some sense of loyalty. But then, that's my opinion. We're always going to see it from our own perspective.'

'How do you know she went to South America?' she said softly. 'Did she come back for you?'

'She sent a postcard once, when I was ten. New continent, new husband, new life. Anyway, after she'd left Earl didn't see the point in paying rent on two places and we moved in to the back of the club. At least I had a roof over my head and food in my belly.'

'A child living in the back of a strip club?' Her eyes changed—ice over fire—and she exhaled sharply. 'The authorities? Didn't they ever catch up with Earl?'

He shrugged, remembering times when he'd been ferried to some stranger's home in the middle of the night. 'Earl was clever. Always one step ahead. It wasn't so bad,' he went on. 'The girls used to make me breakfast sometimes before they went home. They helped me with my homework. Substitute mums of sorts.'

'Your young life must have been very confusing. How did you cope with it all?'

He wrapped a hand around the back of his neck. 'Kept to myself. Studied. Swore one day I'd get out. I was seventeen when I left and found a part-time job and a room to rent.'

'I'll never understand a mother leaving her own flesh and blood.'

He remembered the despair and heartbreak he'd seen too often in his mother's eyes. The guilt that had tormented his youth. The pain of that rejection and abandonment he'd never really got past. 'Because when she looked at me she saw him.'

'Ah…' She shifted closer, the fresh, untainted scent of her skin filling his nostrils. 'But you're *not* him. And she's missed out on knowing someone amazing.' She combed her fingers over the back of his hair. 'You're kind and generous and thoughtful. You're also a man of integrity, and don't let anyone tell you different or make you feel less or they'll have me to deal with.'

A band tightened around his heart. Even knowing his past, she didn't judge. 'Using my inheritance to pay for a safe house is one way of addressing the injustice. My mother didn't benefit, but others will.'

'You're one special guy, you know that?' Her compassionate blue gaze cleared and brightened, and she touched the side of his face with gentle fingers.

He hauled her against him so he could feel her generous warmth against the cold. 'I need that shower.' He needed the water's cleansing spray and her caring hands to rid himself of unwanted memories. Memories that no longer had a place in his life. He closed his eyes. 'You want to wash my back?'

'Does that mean I have to get naked too?'

He drew in a breath and opened his eyes. She was smiling. He touched her hair. 'Unless you want to drive home dripping wet or wearing my bathrobe.'

'Yeah, there's that. Whatever would I do if the car broke down on the way?'

Or you could stay here…

Only he didn't say it. She might be ready to hear it now,

but he didn't want rejection of any kind tonight. He undid the top button of her blouse. 'You *want* to get naked too?'

'Try stopping me. You know what?' She pressed her lips to his chest. 'I even have some spare soap left over in my bag from this afternoon's meeting.' She opened her mouth and flicked out her tongue, leaving a damp trail as she worked her way up to his Adam's apple then his chin. 'There's a new fragrance I'm trialling...' She let her hands wander over his hips, drawing tight little circles through the terry towel with her fingers. 'Eygptian nights. Musk and sandalwood.'

'First Tahiti. Now the East. A round-the-world tour, huh?'

She grazed her fingers over his hardening erection. 'More like a journey of discovery,' she whispered, drawing the towel away. 'Just the two of us.' She reached behind her neck, unfastening her zip and sliding it down so that her dress slipped to the floor. Stepped out of her panties and unsnapped her bra, tossed it away. 'One back scrub coming up.'

At Emma's place later that evening, Jake worked with her on a website design for Naturally Emma. They drank instant coffee and ordered business cards and composed her website pages. It helped take their minds off the earlier conversation. There was a new understanding, a comfortable silence between them as they worked.

Emma took shots of her products for Jake to upload to her computer. She was literally bouncing off the walls with enthusiasm. And nerves. 'Where will I put the extra stock?'

'You'll find a place. I have an empty room under the house if you need it.'

'What if this thing explodes? How will I keep up?'

'Now, *that's* the confidence I like to hear.' He smiled at her, the computer screen's glow reflecting the encouragement etched on his expression. 'You'll give up your day job and employ someone to help you.' He stretched his arms over his head, then reached out to take her hand. 'You'll be fine. If you need help I'm here.'

She breathed deep. 'You don't know how much it means to have you in on this with me, if only to get me started.'

As usual, he shrugged off the praise. 'No worries. I'll have the website ready for you to look at tomorrow night.'

When Jake left, she worked on into the wee hours. She made a start on some mini soap samples and selected a collection for display.

The following day Emma took off in her lunchbreak to slip further down the mall and make arrangements with the shop, collected her business cards from the printer, then caught up with Jake in the evening and approved the website.

Naturally Emma. She stared at the screen, biting her lips, hardly able to believe it was really happening. The lavender background with elegant flowing script and artistic design. The photos. The little piece about her background and qualifications that she'd composed.

'Only two nights to go,' she said, hugging her arms.

'I'll be here to pick you up,' he said, rising. 'But I need to get going. I've got some of my own work to catch up on.'

'I'm sorry. I've monopolised your time.'

'Not at all. Glad I could help.' He pulled her up for a quick kiss. 'Get some sleep.'

The mall was bustling with late-night shoppers when Emma and Jake carried her boxes in at five-thirty on Friday evening. Lights gleamed on the shiny store windows, the smell of roasting nuts and popcorn mingled with perfumes and hair treatments. Elevator music tinkled in the background, along with the ever-present underlying tide of urban chatter.

Kelsey, the shop's proprietor, had set up a table for the products just inside the entrance, and was serving a customer as they arrived. She smiled and waved when she saw them.

'I've got a severe case of killer butterflies,' Emma told Jake as she pulled stock from her box and began arranging it on the table. Her hands weren't steady, her pulse was galloping, and she really, really wanted something to moisten her dust-dry throat. 'What if no one stops by?'

'Looking at you, why wouldn't they?'

She glanced at Jake over her box. He was smiling at her, his eyes full of encouragement. He believed in her, she couldn't let him down. She couldn't let herself down. 'I'd rather they look at the products, but thanks.' She swallowed. 'Would you mind getting me a bottle of water? I forgot mine.'

'Sure.' He put down the box he'd been emptying. 'Back in a moment.'

Kelsey, with curly red hair and moss-green eyes behind her rimless glasses, stepped up as Jake walked away. 'Your guy's a superstar.'

Her guy. Emma started to deny it then stopped. Her heart took a flying leap. Yes, she realised. He was. 'None of it would've happened without his support.' She drew out a cellophane-wrapped basket full of soaps and held it out. 'This is for you. You can take them home, give them to friends. Whatever. I hope your new venture's a success.'

'Oh, Emma, thank you. It's beautiful.' Kelsey admired the basket with a smile, turned it in her hands. 'I think we'll both do well. People look for natural products these days. I'll leave it here for now, so customers can see it. Thanks so much. Oh, I've got a customer...'

Jake slowed as he arrived back, then stopped, watching Emma talk to a couple of elderly ladies. The shop's down-lights glinted on her glossy dark hair. She wore the same white top she'd worn for the hens' night, with a slim white knee-length skirt. Tasteful, professional. A chunky gold bracelet jangled on one wrist as she gesticulated.

She'd ditched the nerves, obviously, and was deep in animated conversation, smiling, eyes alive with friendly interest. Calm, in control, and the sexiest girl in the mall. In all of Australia. How different was this Emma from the Emma he'd seen wearing that top only two weeks ago?

He felt a twinge around his heart—he seemed to be getting a lot of those lately—and his fingers tightened on the red foil balloon with its twirling ribbons he'd purchased on impulse after remembering her edict about no flowers.

He shook his head. No matter what she said, Emma was a woman made for hearts and flowers and pretty words, and he was discovering, to his surprise, that he wanted very badly to give them to her. Because, unlike with his previous lovers, with Emma they would mean something more than traditional and often empty gestures.

He watched her pack soaps into a bag, pass it to one of the women with a smile as they handed over their cash. They continued down the mall. Then a guy in a snazzy business suit stopped at her table.

Jake watched Emma smile some more. Watched her flick back her hair as she talked. Pretty boy leaned closer, head tilted to one side, listening. Nodding. He picked up a soap flower and held it to his nose.

Jake scowled and wasted no time making his way to her table. 'Sorry I took so long, honey.' Slight emphasis on the endearment as he handed her the balloon and her water, then nodded at Mr Businessman. 'How's it going, mate?' He stuck out his hand. 'Jake Carmody. Emma's accountant.'

The man shook his hand. 'Daniel McDougal.'

Beside Jake, Emma made a noise at the back of her throat, setting water and balloon aside. 'Thanks.' Then she darted him a disconcerted glance. 'Jake, Daniel is from Brisbane. He owns a large health food chain and is interested in trialling my products up there.'

'That sounds great.' Jake nodded again. 'I'll let you two get on with it, then.' He dropped a firm hand on Emma's shoulder, let it linger a few seconds longer than necessary. 'If you need me, my phone's on. I'll be back to help you pack up.'

'My accountant?' Emma said on the way home.

'Yeah.' Why the hell had he got so proprietorial back there? He didn't *do* proprietorial. He dismissed the unsettling notion from his mind and concentrated on the traffic. 'Because I'm coming over on Monday night to look over your financial records,' he said. If this was going to take off, Emma needed someone she trusted from the get-go to help her manage the financial side.

'Oh. Okay. Thanks.' She bopped her little balloon against his arm. 'And thank you for tonight.'

'Pleasure.'

He glanced her way. She had a dreamy expression on her face. He looked away quickly. *Accountant? Sure.* She knew exactly what had gone through his mind.

On Saturday Emma caught up with all the things she hadn't been doing, such as grocery shopping, washing and cleaning. In the evening Jake took her to a little out-of-the-way café where the pasta was hot and the jazz was cool.

She was thrilled when Jake asked her to share dog-walking duties the following morning. They took Seeker for his walk before Jake went in to the office to catch up on his own neglected work.

Emma spent the afternoon looking forward to seeing him again at dinner while she put together a gourmet beef casserole and whipped up a batch of Jake's favourite lemon poppyseed cakes.

But how long would this thing with Jake last? How long before he tired of her? The way her father had tired of her mother and taken a mistress. The way Wayne had tired of her and found Rani. A guy like Jake with good-looks and all the charisma in the world could have any woman he wanted.

He'd never mentioned anything lasting. *Don't look too far ahead,* he'd told her. *Enjoy the ride.*

And it was one amazing ride.

She could handle it if—when—it came time to let go. Whatever happened, she'd be fine. Because he'd changed her, made her a confident woman who could meet life head-on. She loved him. But a wise woman knew if her love wasn't returned there was nowhere for it to go. She hoped she was strong enough now to let him move on. At some point.

She needed to stand on her own two feet with this business. And she could. He'd given her the belief in herself to give it a really good go. After he'd shown her what to do with the accounting side of things she was going to say thank you very much and be her own businesswoman.

When Jake arrived after work on Monday night, Emma was looking more than a little harassed.

At the front door they spent a moment with their lips locked before she broke away with a sigh. 'This is impossible,' she said, walking to her work spot at the dining room table. She flicked at an untidy pile of papers, sending a couple sailing to the floor. 'I can't do figures. It's a mess.'

'First off—calm down.' He took her hands in his. 'I'm in business law. That makes me a figures guy. Brew us a coffee while I look over your books.'

She stared up at him, eyes panicked. 'Books? I don't have books. I have paper. Piles and piles of paper.'

'Okay. Why don't *I* make us coffee while you gather them together? Then I can take a look. And don't worry. That's what I'm here for.'

'But it's *not* your worry. I have to be able to do it on my own…'

She trailed off, but not before he heard the hiccup in her voice. A sombre mood fell over him, a dark cloud on a still darker night. He squeezed her hands that little bit firmer. 'I'll be available for however long you need my help.'

She looked away at the clutter on the table. 'I'm not a complete moron. I should be able to handle it myself.'

'You're not and you will,' he reassured her. 'I'll sort it, show you how it all works, then you can take over.'

A few hours later he'd organised her paper filing system into some sort of order. He'd set up an accounting program on her laptop and entered her details. All he had left then was to show her how to manage it.

He'd hardly been aware, but at some point she'd finished packing and stacking and made another coffee. He sipped his, found it stone cold. Stretching out the kinks in his spine and neck, he turned to see her zonked out on the couch, fast asleep, a book on the Pitfalls and Perils of Small Business still open on her stomach.

He didn't get nearly enough time to watch her in that state, so he took the opportunity while it presented itself. Turning his chair around, he straddled it, resting his forearms along the back.

Her waterfall of glossy dark hair tumbled over the side of the couch. Her long, dark eyelashes rested on pale cheeks. Her mouth…a thing of beauty, full and plump and turned up ever so slightly at the corners, as if waiting for one chaste kiss to awaken her…

Her eyes would open and that glorious sapphire gaze would fix on his and he'd kiss her again…not so chaste this time…

His lips tingled with sweet promise. His heart beat faster, re-energising his bloodstream, reawakening sluggish muscles. Desire unfurled deep in his belly. Amazing—this feeling, this need for her, never waned. In fact, it was stronger than ever.

But he touched only her silky hair. She needed her sleep. She looked pale, worn out. He should leave, let her rest. They'd catch up tomorrow. But he couldn't leave her to finish the night on that spring-worn couch.

Gathering her in his arms, he carried her to bed, laid her down, and for his own peace of mind pulled the quilt right up to her chin.

She stirred and looked up at him through sleepy eyes…

And it was as if he saw all the days and nights in a fantasy-filled future when he'd wake and lose his heart over and over every time he gazed into those captivating blue depths—

When I saw my children in her eyes…

A bowling ball rolled through his chest. His throat tightened as if the air was slowly being squeezed out of him by an iron fist, and for a few crazy seconds he thought he might black out.

But his moment of panic slid away like an outgoing tide over hard-packed sand, replaced by a shiny and unfamiliar warmth which seeped deep into his heart.

Love.

It had to be love. What else could it be? He'd not recognised it before because he'd never experienced it. Never believed in it. Not for him. Love had always been an unknown. His childhood had been one of rejection and indifference. His entire adult existence had revolved around relationships that never lasted. The women in his life had been about fun and good times. He'd never really taken the time to get to know them on a deeper level. Hadn't wanted to. Maybe he'd been afraid to.

But he knew Emma. And she'd opened his eyes and his heart to a different world. A world where life held more meaning than he'd ever imagined.

'Jake... Wha...?' Her drowsy murmur drifted away.

'Sleep, sweetheart,' he murmured against her temple, and she snuggled into her pillow, eyes already closed again.

He woke before dawn, still fully dressed on top of her quilt, his eyes snapping open to the fading sound of a car's tyres screeching in the distance. Emma was spooned against him as warm and soft as a kitten. He shifted carefully off her bed and let himself out into the pearl-grey of early morning.

He hurried to his car. He had plans to make before his working day started.

CHAPTER FOURTEEN

JAKE was wearing a groove in the floorboards in Emma's studio. He'd left the office at lunchtime, dropped by Emma's workplace and asked her for a key so he could work on her computer. She'd told him she'd be home by six.

It was now twenty minutes past.

The mustard chicken and orzo casserole he'd ordered from his favourite gourmet kitchen was in the oven. A bottle of her favourite bubbly was chilling in the fridge, along with a couple of his favourite gourmet cupcakes.

He'd cleared the work from her table and covered its scarred surface with a cream lace cloth he'd found in her kitchen drawer, placed on it a bunch of red poppies he'd bought.

Should he have taken her to some fancy restaurant instead? No. He didn't want a bunch of strangers intruding. He wanted to share the moment with her. Only her.

A beam of light arced through the window and the familiar engine's sound had him reaching for gas lighter and candles.

Grabbing the plastic carry bag of fried chicken and a bottle of fizzy stuff from the passenger seat, Emma swung her bag over her shoulder and almost danced down the steps.

She couldn't wait to tell him her news. She hadn't phoned. She needed to say it in person.

'Honey, I'm home,' she sing-songed as she pushed the door open.

She was met by some herby, aromatic fragrance. On the table, tall red poppies speared out of a jar alongside two squat red candles already lit.

Jake was pouring fine pink champagne into two glasses that were far too elegant to have come from her cupboard. *He* looked too elegant, in slim-fitting black trousers and a snowy-white shirt that looked as if it had just come out of a box.

'Seems you beat me to it.' She set down her own cheap bottle of fizz on the sideboard and admired the candlelight reflecting on crystal and silver. 'This looks wickedly romantic.'

'I thought it was time I took a chance on the romance bit. You don't mind, do you?' Hands occupied with wine and glasses, he grinned and leaned forward so that she could plant an enthusiastic kiss on his lips. He smelled of some exotic new fragrance.

'I don't mind. Taking chances is what it's all about, right?' Overflowing with excitement, she sashayed over to the oven, peeked at the delicious-looking meal inside. 'And I bought take-away. You should've let me know you were planning a seduction.'

'I wanted to surprise you.'

'You did. And I've got—'

'Everything's ready. Sit.'

He didn't appear to hear her. Okay, this wasn't the moment, she decided. He'd obviously gone to a lot of trouble. 'It smells yummy.'

'It tastes even better.' Pulling out her chair, he waited till she was seated, then walked to the oven. He removed the casserole, set it on the table, then sat down opposite her.

'You okay?' She studied him. 'You seem a little...' she circled a finger in the air '...preoccupied.'

His mouth kicked up at one corner as his gaze drifted over the front of her shirt. 'If I am, it's your fault for looking so sexy after a day at work.'

'And don't you know just the right things to say?' While he spooned the meal into shallow bowls, she fingered a poppy. 'I didn't know poppies had blue centres.'

'These do.'

'Made-to-order poppies? Hmm. You *have* put thought into this.'

'They remind me of you in that sexy red coat of yours. Tall, slim. Blue-eyed. Gorgeous.' He raised their glasses, handed her one. 'To happiness.' Did his eyes look different tonight? Deep and dark... Maybe she was imagining it.

Because everything looked different tonight. From the sunset to the sea, even her old studio apartment. Everything *felt* different tonight. Her life was about to change.

'To happiness.' She took a sip, then set her glass down. She was bursting to talk but she squashed it. She didn't want to spoil his evening's plans. She wanted him to see her make time and enjoy the meal he'd obviously taken so much thought with first. The crystal flutes were sparkly new and very expensive. He'd used her best silver cutlery and china and her grandmother's tablecloth.

She spread a matching cloth napkin over her knee. 'Did you cook this yourself?'

'It's from a gourmet shop in Bondi. I shop there so often the owner's thinking of making me a partner.' He passed her a bowl. 'I'd have cooked, but today's been a bit of a rush.'

So while they ate she asked him about his day. One of his colleagues in the office was taking on a high-profile case. He'd almost finished entering her data on the computer.

How was it going with Cherry and Kevin? He'd driven Cherry to the safe house and they'd chosen paint for the walls. Cherry and a couple of the other girls were starting that job next week in their spare time.

When they'd polished off the last cake crumb from their plates and were enjoying their filtered coffee, Jake decided the moment was right now. He took a gulp of coffee to moisten his throat and steady his nerves. His fingers tightened on the little box in his trouser pocket.

'Emma, I—'

'I have some news—'

Both spoke at the same time.

She was clutching her hands together beneath her chin. Her sapphire eyes shone like stars, reflecting the candlelight.

A premonition snaked down Jake's spine and his breath snagged in his chest. Why did he suddenly feel as if the floor was about to give way? He nodded once. 'You first.'

Her shoulders lifted and she leaned forward. Her familiar fragrance curled around his nostrils.

'You talked about taking a chance earlier—on romance. And it's been lovely. Everything. Thank you for making the evening so special.'

He acknowledged that, but didn't speak.

'I've taken a chance too. I've been offered work in Queensland. *Real* work. Work I love, work I've wanted all my life but never had the opportunity to do.'

Jake was having trouble processing the words. *Queensland.* He was grateful he was sitting down because his legs suddenly felt like lead stumps. 'Queensland?'

'I know. Isn't it exciting? I can't believe it.'

Neither could Jake. 'Where? Who? You've made plans?' *Without discussing it with me?*

'You remember Daniel McDougal? From the mall last week? Well, he was so impressed with my products he had them analysed and everything, consulted with his partners, and rang me this afternoon. He wants to invest in my product line *and* take me on as a consultant to liaise with his client base all around the state.'

Daniel McDougal. Mr Pretty Boy. 'But what do you know about him? Aren't you jumping in without the facts? God, Emma, you can't just—'

'Turns out he's Kelsey's cousin. You know—the owner of the shop? I talked to her, and checked him out on the internet to make sure. Danny's a real success story up there.'

So it was *Danny* now? Jake clenched his jaw. 'You don't have to make a decision right away, Emma.' But she didn't seem to be listening.

'He's got stores around Australia. He's booked me an airline ticket for tomorrow morning to meet the staff and look over the factory before I commit to anything. He emailed me the information. I have a copy right here. Since you're the expert, I'd be grateful if you'd check it out?' She reached into her bag, pulled some papers out, set them on the table.

Damn right he'd check it out. He picked them up with a restraint he was far from feeling. 'This isn't something you simply say yes to, Emma.' He flicked through the first couple of pages. 'There are other considerations to take into account.' *Us, for starters.*

'Of course, and I know that. Jake, put those pages down and look at me.'

He did. He'd never seen her so happy. That sparkle in her eyes, excitement glowing in her cheeks.

'We've got something special,' she said. 'But it was only ever temporary, I'm realistic enough to know that. I'm a career girl, you said so yourself. This chance to do something meaningful with my life is what I've been waiting for. And if it wasn't for you I'd never have had the courage to go for it. I have to try or it'll all have been for nothing. Do you understand?'

His fingers clenched beneath the table. 'Yes.' She was thinking with her head, not her heart—she was doing the right thing. He knew she had to give it a shot. Because if he told her he loved her and asked her to stay and she missed out on her big opportunity he'd never forgive himself. He forced himself to smile. 'I'm proud of you, Emma. You've come so far.'

Her answering smile and the dancing sapphires in her eyes faded a little. 'It's such a big decision, and I have to make it on my own, but… Oh, Jake, I…' She bit down on her lip. 'I…I almost wish I could ask you to make the decision for me. *With* me.'

Damn. Her heart was bleeding into the mix, threatening to sabotage everything. He needed to leave soon, because he didn't trust himself not to try and change her mind— and that would be the worst thing he could ever do for her.

'That's the old Emma talking. Don't listen to her. You know what you want, so go for it.'

A memory of his mother flashed through his mind. She'd left him too. The circumstances were at opposite ends of the spectrum but the hurt was the same. All these years he'd never allowed a woman into his heart, and in a couple of weeks Emma had managed to do what no other woman had.

'Emma. You're a very special woman and I've enjoyed being with you. But circumstances seem to have made the decision for us. And I want you to go. I want you to have that opportunity to shine because I know you will.'

Rising, he swiped his jacket that hung over a chair, shrugged it on—he'd never felt so cold. He picked up her papers. 'I'll look this over and get back to you.'

'Jake, wait.' She pushed up, eyes wide. 'Why are you leaving so soon? Didn't you have something you wanted to tell me just now? You let me have my say—it's your turn.'

He shook his head. 'I was going to tell you I'm flying out too—tomorrow morning. A client's set up a new business in Melbourne and wants my advice.' He waved a hand over the table. 'The meal was to…sweeten things.' He smiled again but it felt as if his lips had turned to stone. 'Turns out it was a celebration after all. And if I know anything about women, you'll need the rest of the night to sort what you're taking and pack.'

He took her in his arms, kissed her beautiful lips just once. Inhaled the scent of her shampoo, drifted his fingers over her silky cheeks as he stepped back and looked into her eyes one last time.

'Go, Emma, and make me proud.'

CHAPTER FIFTEEN

Emma yawned as the taxi pulled into her driveway at ten p.m. on Thursday evening. She paid the cabbie, jumped out to key in the gate's security code, then collected her cabin bag from the footpath.

As she rolled it across the pavers she saw her mother exit the back door, the old cardigan she'd wrapped around her shoulders flapping in the breeze as she came to meet her.

Just what she didn't need right now, but Emma pasted on a smile. 'Hi, Mum. You're back.'

'Yesterday. I got your text. How was Brisbane?'

'Warm and sticky.' And lonely.

'Jake dropped by this afternoon to drop this off for you.' She held out a large envelope. 'Said he'd rather leave it with me than in the letterbox.'

'Thanks.' She frowned. 'I thought he was going to Melbourne.' It must have only been an overnight stay. Emma knew she should wait until she was alone, but she needed to see what Jake thought of the offer of employment. She so needed to see his handwriting. Anything. Something of him.

She slid the documents out. A green sticky note was attached to the top page.

Hi Em. Looks OK.
Remember, go with your gut—if you think it's right,
do it. And good luck.
J.

'My offer of employment.'

Emma blinked back tears as she slid the contents back into the envelope. Forty-eight hours ago she'd thought it was worth more than gold. Now she knew it wasn't. A successful career was an empty one if she couldn't share it with the man she loved.

Rubbing the chill air from her arms, she reached for the handle of her case. 'I hope you were pleasant to Jake?'

Her mother pursed her lips, but then seemed to relax a little, and something like a smile twitched at her lips. 'Bit of a charmer, that one. Done all right for himself, hasn't he?'

'Yes. He has.'

'Come inside for a few moments.' She turned and began walking the way she'd come.

The kitchen, when Emma entered, was warm and smelled of fresh-baked cinnamon cake. She hadn't smelled that comfortable homey aroma in this kitchen in years.

Her mother pulled a carton of milk from the fridge. 'Would you like a hot chocolate? I could do with one myself.'

'Thanks.' Emma sat down at the kitchen table. 'You've been baking.'

'Stan's coming up to Sydney tomorrow.' She put milk in the microwave, then set slices of fresh buttered cake on the table. 'Try this and tell me if I got it right. I tried a new recipe.'

Emma took a slice and broke a piece off, bit into it.

'Mmm—yum.' She dusted off her fingers. 'So how long will Stan be staying?'

'Not sure yet.'

'He's staying here?'

'Yes.' Her mother stirred chocolate powder into the hot milk and poured it into two mugs, then carried them to the table and sat down.

Emma cupped her hands around the mug and blew on the steaming surface. 'This smells good.' Almost as good as the old milk and honey fix. 'So...things are going well for you two?'

'We have a lot in common.'

'That's great, Mum. What are you planning while he's here?'

'We'll take it as it comes. What about you and Jake?'

Emma could feel her mother's eyes on her and stared into her mug. 'He... We...' She swallowed the lump that rose up her throat.

'He was the mistake you thought he might be?'

Still staring at her mug, she said, 'It was one of those get-it-out-of-your-system things...' Only she hadn't.

'So you're going to Brisbane to work?'

'I thought I was. But I've changed my mind.'

She flashed Emma a look. 'Why?'

'Mum, why did you stay with Dad when you had so many reasons not to?'

'I had two children.'

Emma's jaw tightened. 'And you made us pay for your unhappiness. Every day of our lives.'

She saw her mother flinch, then she put her mug down and folded her arms on the edge of the table. 'Yes. I did. I'm sorry for it. I was wrong.'

Emma studied her, thoughtful. Jake's mother had abandoned her child and he'd suffered the consequences his whole life. Emma's had stayed, even if it would have been better for all if she hadn't. But maybe her mother had been too afraid to leave—afraid of the changes it would bring. The way Emma had been afraid.

Basically her mother had made what she'd thought was the right decision, and it wasn't Emma's place to judge.

'Sorry, I shouldn't have said that,' Emma murmured.

'It needed to be said. I needed to hear it. But a good man, a man who takes the time to look beneath the hard shell and find the woman inside screaming to be let out...' Her mother's voice softened. It was a tone Emma hadn't thought her capable of, and an unexpected smile brightened her whole demeanour. 'Well, he can change your life.'

Emma nodded. 'Yes. He can.' Stan had instigated the change in her mum without Bernice even being aware of it. And wasn't that what Jake had done for Emma?

Friday

'Good afternoon, Carmody and Associates.'

'Hi, Jasmine, it's Emma Byrne.'

'Emma, hi.' There was a smile in Jake's PA's voice that wasn't only professional courtesy. 'What can I do for you?'

Emma's fingers tightened on the phone and she rolled her lips together before saying, 'I was wondering...is Jake there?

'Yes. He's free at the moment. Do you want me to put you thr—?'

'No.' She swallowed. 'Thanks. I wanted to know... I want...' She sucked in a deep breath. 'Actually, I was hoping you could help me...'

Jake checked his watch, then pressed the intercom. 'Jasmine? Looks like your friend's a no-show. Why don't you give him a call, tell him to reschedule? I'm knocking off early—'

'She'll be here,' she assured him. 'Do me a favour and wait a few more moments.'

Jake was already shutting down his computer with his free hand. Jasmine hadn't mentioned her friend was a woman. The only woman he wanted to see walking through that door was a million miles away.

'I gave her my word you'd see her tonight,' Jasmine continued. 'Hang on...' He heard a muffled sound then, 'I can see her from the window. She's walking into the building now.'

Emma refused to let the nerves zapping beneath her ribcage win. She was a woman on a mission and nothing was going to stand in her way. So she wasn't afraid of walking into an office high-rise to face the most important meeting of her life.

Six p.m. on a chilly autumn evening in Sydney's CBD and the business day was over. Workers were trickling out of the building on their way home.

Her work was just beginning. The most important work she'd ever done. The most important work she'd ever do. She'd promised herself she'd talk to Jake Carmody, and she would. She could.

Shrugging her bag higher, she marched inside. A couple of men in snazzy business suits exited the lift. She clutched the miniature hat box at her waist as she passed them. Did they know her life was on a cliff's edge? Could they hear how hard her heart was pounding? She hit the button for the fourteenth floor and watched the numbers light up while her stomach stayed on the ground floor.

The doors slid open smoothly and she stepped out. Jasmine looked up and smiled, collecting her bag from her desk on her way out. 'Go straight in. He's getting a little impatient.'

'Thanks.'

Emma heard him on the phone before she reached the open door. That deep, lazy voice that rolled over her senses like caramel sauce. Only three days, but she'd missed hearing that voice. She loved that voice. She loved the man it belonged to. It was time she took the big, scary leap and let him in on that fact.

She took a fortifying breath, then knocked and entered.

He was sitting behind his desk and looked up sharply, eyes widening when she closed the door behind her.

'Something's come up. I'll speak to you tomorrow,' he said into his mobile without taking his eyes off her. He disconnected and set the phone on the desk. 'Emma.'

'Hello, Jake.'

'I'm expecting a client…' He studied her face. 'I'm guessing it's you.'

'Jasmine told me you'd be here. She asked you to wait, so thank you.'

His eyes raked over her coat and she felt a flush rise up her neck. Heat, desire, longing. Her body reacted to his gaze as if it had been programmed for his exclusive use, and her nipples hardened beneath her finely woven cashmere jumper. She wished she knew what he was thinking, how he felt about her turning up without calling first.

He checked his watch. 'I was about to leave. I need to get home.'

Her heart clenched so tight she wondered that her blood still pumped around her body. Her fingers tightened so hard on the little box she wondered it didn't implode. 'A… date?' She had to force the words out.

He stared at her with those beautiful, dark, unreadable eyes. 'What do you think, Emma?'

'I think…if it was…I'd try to talk you into cancelling because I need to talk to you first.'

'No need—there is no date.' He was turning his mobile over and over in his hands. Watching her. 'How was Brisbane? Is the new job everything you wanted?'

'Yes. And no.' She focused on those eyes. 'It's everything I wanted in a career. Double the income I'm making at the call centre. A spacious office with my name on the door. The chance to build my own business on the side. A chance to travel.' She sucked in her lips. 'But it's not enough.'

'Not enough.' Rising, he came around to her side of the desk, leaned his backside against the edge. 'Why isn't it enough, Em?'

He enjoyed being with her, she knew that. He made love to her as if she were a goddess. He believed in her. But did he love her? How would he respond if she asked him? There were no guarantees in life and love, but wasn't taking that leap of faith what it was all about?

She tightened her fingers on the little box and sucked in a lungful of air. 'It's not enough because I want more. I want it all. What's the point in being successful if you're lonely?' She pushed her gift into his hands. 'I love you, Jake. I need you in my life. No matter what else I do or don't have, I need you.'

He shook his head slightly, as if he couldn't believe what he was hearing, then looked down at the box. Back to her.

'Open it.'

She forgot to breathe as he lifted the lid. He met her eyes. A slow smile curved his lips and her breath whooshed out. He lifted out the cupcake with its red heart piped on top.

'It's not soap. It's chocolate—you can eat this one.'

'I'm not so sure I want to. It's too special.'

She twisted her trembling fingers together in front of her. 'Jake...do you love me back? I really, really need to know if I'm making an idiot of myself here...'

'Emma.' He set the cake and its box beside him on the desk, then covered her hands with his. 'I know that when I'm with you, when I look at you, I have this feeling inside me that makes Everest seem like an ant hill. It makes me want to go out and climb its highest peak with my bare hands. It gives me a reason to get up and watch the sun rise and thank the universe for bringing you into my life. I'd say that's love, wouldn't you?'

'Yes. Because that's how you make me feel too.' She was beyond terrified that she might have let this chance slip through her hands. It gave her strength to continue. 'I came here to say...to ask...Jake, will you marry me?' The last words rushed out on a trembling breath.

His eyes darkened, warmed. And his slow smile was the most wonderful, heartbreakingly beautiful sight she'd ever seen. 'That's going to be one hell of a story to tell our children some day.'

Our children. Her heart blossomed with all the possibilities of a future together opening up inside her. 'So...is that a yes?'

He brushed the back of his hand over her cheek, the side of her neck, leaving a shimmer of heat, the scent of his skin. 'I'm not planning on having our kids out of wedlock, sweetheart.'

He bent his head towards her and she rose on tiptoe, slid her arms around his neck and pressed her lips to his with all the pent-up emotion and love she had inside her. He kissed her back without hesitation, without reservation, dragging her close so that she could feel the fast, hard beat of his heart against hers.

Finally she drew back so she could see him, cupped

his treasured face in her hands. 'I was afraid to love you. Afraid of its power. It can lift you up, but it can bury you so deep you can't see a way out. I saw what it did to my mother. I saw how she let it destroy her.

'But when I went to Brisbane I realised I wasn't like her. You showed me that, by pushing me out of my comfort zone and allowing me to see another side of myself. And I want to thank you for the rest of our lives.'

He smiled down at her. 'And I want to let you.' Then his expression sobered. 'I was afraid too, but wouldn't admit it—even to myself. I've never let anyone close. It was easier to play the field and move on. But with you I couldn't seem to let you go. Until you told me about the new job. I wanted you to have that career you worked so hard for. That success. I had to let you go and find it for yourself, even though I knew I loved you.'

'It's not enough. Not without you.' She tugged his hand. 'Can we get out of here?'

'Sure thing.' Tightening their clasped fingers, he headed for the door. 'I've got a surprise for you.'

Jake handed his address and a healthy wad of notes to the parking attendant on their way to pick up Emma's car. 'Find someone to take care of it and there's enough cash for a cab back,' he told him, then, slinging his arm around Emma's shoulders, he hustled her along the street. He wondered that his feet touched the ground. Half an hour ago he'd been at the lowest point in his life and now he was flying.

A short time later he kissed her on the front door step. 'Welcome home. I love you, Emma, and I'm never going to tire of hearing myself say it.'

'I'm never going to tire of h—' A long, low whine interrupted, vibrating through the door, followed by a whimper and a series of sharp barks. '*What* is that?'

He unlocked the door and a flurry of paws and joyous barks greeted them. 'Meet Scratch.'

'You bought a dog? So *that's* why you had to get home.'

'He's the abandoned dog I told you about.'

'And you rescued him.'

'I just couldn't bring myself to leave him at the shelter, so I picked him up yesterday.' He bent to scratch behind his silky ears. 'I think we rescued each other—didn't we, boy?'

'We were all in need of rescue,' Emma murmured. 'Hey, there, you little cutie, you.'

Jake watched her wasting no time getting acquainted, crouching down so Scratch could sniff her and approve. With a joyous yelp he rolled onto his back, his tongue lolling out, adoration in his eyes.

Jake squatted beside Emma to scratch the dog's tummy. 'So what do you think—you and me and a crazy pooch? You didn't know he was part of the deal—you sure you still want to marry me?'

'Are you kidding? He seals the deal absolutely.'

He looked at Emma, his heart overflowing with that mysterious thing called love. It had eluded him all his life but now… Now he had it all.

A few moments later, with Scratch tucking into his dinner, Jake put the little velvet box into Emma's hands. 'To make it official.'

Her eyes widened. 'What's this? How…?'

'I was going to propose to you the other night. Until you told me your news.'

Realisation dawned in her bright blue eyes. 'So *that's* why you went to so much effort. Oh, Jake. I was so focused on myself I didn't—'

He placed a finger on her lips. 'Just open it.'

'Oh, my…' she breathed. 'It's beautiful.'

Three diamonds on a platinum band winked in the light. 'One for you, one for me, one for the kids we're going to make,' he told her, sliding it onto her finger.

He lifted her off the floor, twirled her around and around until they were both dizzy, then waltzed her to his bedroom the way he'd waltzed her to bed that first time they'd made love.

He tugged on her belt. 'I'll have you know the first time I saw you in that coat I wondered what you were hiding beneath it. Now...take it off and let me see.'

Later, Emma cuddled against him in his king-size bed. Scratch snored doggy snores in his basket nearby. 'I think I'd like to stay right here for the rest of the weekend.' She stretched, feeling satisfied, in love, and entirely too lazy.

'Sounds like a plan. But I doubt Scratch will agree.'

'Our house by the sea and a dog,' she murmured. 'This really is home. What a wonderful life...'

'And what do you want to do with that life...' he nuzzled the sweet taste of her breast '...besides making love endlessly till dawn?'

'I want to concentrate on Naturally Emma. Danny's still going to market my products in Queensland, and I might go up once a month to see how it's going.'

'Maybe I can accompany you sometimes. As your accountant.'

'Nuh-uh. If you accompany me it'll be as my husband.'

'Even better.' His hand created a warm friction over her belly. 'I'm shifting some of my office work home. When I decided to take on a dog I made the commitment to be home more.'

'We'll neither of us ever get any work done.' She drew a line up his shin with her toes and draped her top half over him like a scarf.

His laugh was more of a choke as his arms went around her to pull her all the way on top. 'Reckon you're right.'

She buried her face in the musky warmth of his neck and breathed in his scent. 'I'm always right. I asked you to marry me, didn't I?'

'So...how does a wedding as soon as Ry and Stella come back from their honeymoon sound?'

She lifted her head so she could look into those warm coffee eyes and see his love for her shining through. 'Perfect.'

* * * * *

ROMANCE

A Vow of Obligation	Lynne Graham
Defying Drakon	Carole Mortimer
Playing the Greek's Game	Sharon Kendrick
One Night in Paradise	Maisey Yates
His Majesty's Mistake	Jane Porter
Duty and the Beast	Trish Morey
The Darkest of Secrets	Kate Hewitt
Behind the Castello Doors	Chantelle Shaw
The Morning After The Wedding Before	Anne Oliver
Never Stay Past Midnight	Mira Lyn Kelly
Valtieri's Bride	Caroline Anderson
Taming the Lost Prince	Raye Morgan
The Nanny Who Kissed Her Boss	Barbara McMahon
Falling for Mr Mysterious	Barbara Hannay
One Day to Find a Husband	Shirley Jump
The Last Woman He'd Ever Date	Liz Fielding
Sydney Harbour Hospital: Lexi's Secret	Melanie Milburne
West Wing to Maternity Wing!	Scarlet Wilson

HISTORICAL

Lady Priscilla's Shameful Secret	Christine Merrill
Rake with a Frozen Heart	Marguerite Kaye
Miss Cameron's Fall from Grace	Helen Dickson
Society's Most Scandalous Rake	Isabelle Goddard

MEDICAL

Diamond Ring for the Ice Queen	Lucy Clark
No.1 Dad in Texas	Dianne Drake
The Dangers of Dating Your Boss	Sue MacKay
The Doctor, His Daughter and Me	Leonie Knight

Mills & Boon® Large Print
May 2012

ROMANCE

The Man Who Risked It All — Michelle Reid
The Sheikh's Undoing — Sharon Kendrick
The End of her Innocence — Sara Craven
The Talk of Hollywood — Carole Mortimer
Master of the Outback — Margaret Way
Their Miracle Twins — Nikki Logan
Runaway Bride — Barbara Hannay
We'll Always Have Paris — Jessica Hart

HISTORICAL

The Lady Confesses — Carole Mortimer
The Dangerous Lord Darrington — Sarah Mallory
The Unconventional Maiden — June Francis
Her Battle-Scarred Knight — Meriel Fuller

MEDICAL

The Child Who Rescued Christmas — Jessica Matthews
Firefighter With A Frozen Heart — Dianne Drake
Mistletoe, Midwife...Miracle Baby — Anne Fraser
How to Save a Marriage in a Million — Leonie Knight
Swallowbrook's Winter Bride — Abigail Gordon
Dynamite Doc or Christmas Dad? — Marion Lennox

Mills & Boon® Hardback
June 2012

ROMANCE

A Secret Disgrace	Penny Jordan
The Dark Side of Desire	Julia James
The Forbidden Ferrara	Sarah Morgan
The Truth Behind his Touch	Cathy Williams
Enemies at the Altar	Melanie Milburne
A World She Doesn't Belong To	Natasha Tate
In Defiance of Duty	Caitlin Crews
In the Italian's Sights	Helen Brooks
Dare She Kiss & Tell?	Aimee Carson
Waking Up In The Wrong Bed	Natalie Anderson
Plain Jane in the Spotlight	Lucy Gordon
Battle for the Soldier's Heart	Cara Colter
It Started with a Crush...	Melissa McClone
The Navy Seal's Bride	Soraya Lane
My Greek Island Fling	Nina Harrington
A Girl Less Ordinary	Leah Ashton
Sydney Harbour Hospital: Bella's Wishlist	Emily Forbes
Celebrity in Braxton Falls	Judy Campbell

HISTORICAL

The Duchess Hunt	Elizabeth Beacon
Marriage of Mercy	Carla Kelly
Chained to the Barbarian	Carol Townend
My Fair Concubine	Jeannie Lin

MEDICAL

Doctor's Mile-High Fling	Tina Beckett
Hers For One Night Only?	Carol Marinelli
Unlocking the Surgeon's Heart	Jessica Matthews
Marriage Miracle in Swallowbrook	Abigail Gordon

Mills & Boon® Large Print

June 2012

ROMANCE

An Offer She Can't Refuse	Emma Darcy
An Indecent Proposition	Carol Marinelli
A Night of Living Dangerously	Jennie Lucas
A Devilishly Dark Deal	Maggie Cox
The Cop, the Puppy and Me	Cara Colter
Back in the Soldier's Arms	Soraya Lane
Miss Prim and the Billionaire	Lucy Gordon
Dancing with Danger	Fiona Harper

HISTORICAL

The Disappearing Duchess	Anne Herries
Improper Miss Darling	Gail Whitiker
Beauty and the Scarred Hero	Emily May
Butterfly Swords	Jeannie Lin

MEDICAL

New Doc in Town	Meredith Webber
Orphan Under the Christmas Tree	Meredith Webber
The Night Before Christmas	Alison Roberts
Once a Good Girl...	Wendy S. Marcus
Surgeon in a Wedding Dress	Sue MacKay
The Boy Who Made Them Love Again	Scarlet Wilson